A Pink Potion Gone Wrong

A Witch's Cove Mystery
Book 2

Vella Day

A Pink Potion Gone Wrong

Print Edition
www.velladay.com
velladayauthor@gmail.com

Cover Art by Jaycee DeLorenzo
Edited by Rebecca Cartee and Carol Adcock-Bezzo

Published in the United States of America
Print book ISBN: 978-1-951430-07-8

An unlucky witch. A talking pink iguana. A frustrated ghost needing to know who killed him.

Welcome back to Witch's Cove where the people—with the exception of a few random law breakers—are friendly and the sun always shines. If you want to talk to a dead relative, learn about your future, or need a spell created just for you, you've come to the right place.

Hi, I'm Glinda Goodall, and after fourteen years of hearing my iguana complain about how my spell turned his green skin pink, I finally have a chance to help him. The problem? I'm either the worst witch in Florida or the unluckiest. At the store where I buy my potions, the owner happened to be out of town. No worries. Why shouldn't I trust the ancient substitute who is hard of hearing and doesn't see well?

Long story short, she mixed in the wrong ingredient, and instead of turning Iggy back to green, I ended up seeing ghosts! Just my luck, the first semi-translucent figure I ran into was recently murdered and wants my help to figure out who did it. Never one to turn down a soul in need, I agree.

If you want to tag along, please do. You'll find me at the Tiki Hut Grill most days serving breakfast and smiles. Oh, yeah. I found a talking cat too!

Chapter One

If you didn't read book 1 or need to do a quick catch up, check out my website.

velladay.com/mysteries.html

"I'M ON STRIKE," my cute, pink iguana said as he whipped his tail back and forth, digging his claws into the rattan stool he was perched upon. "I'm not helping you with any more cases."

I ignored Iggy, mostly because he was being silly. I'd only been involved in one murder case in my life. But when my familiar was in a bad mood, the best thing to do was give him space to cool down.

To be fair, these last few weeks had been hard on both of us. Me, because I had to help prove that my best male friend's brother didn't kill our not-so-beloved deputy. Iggy had been excited to help solve the crime, but now that the real criminal had been brought to justice, he felt left out. Iggy liked the action.

So why would an adrenaline junkie threaten to boycott the chance to sleuth in the future? I didn't have a clue, but knowing him, he'd reveal his motives eventually.

Just to be clear, this level of frustration wasn't new to him. Iggy was often in a state of despair, mostly because he was pink (long story how that came about). And by a long story, I mean about fourteen years long.

The short of it was that I had conjured him from the Hendrian National Forest when I was only twelve. Considering my inexperience, it shouldn't come as a surprise that I failed to get the black cat I was trying for. Instead, Iggy showed up—and I turned him pink by mistake. Whoops.

For sure, Iggy got the raw end of the deal. I was a terrible witch back then—still am—because I'm bad at doing spells. It was why I try to limit doing them as much as possible.

"Don't you want to know why I won't help you anymore?" he said, his nose pressed against the picture window that faced the Gulf of Mexico.

I already knew. At least I think I did. He'd complained about being pink almost every day. "No."

"Have you ever asked for help regarding my problem?" he asked.

Nailed it!

Clearly, my familiar wasn't going to let it go. I finished my tea, set it down on the coffee table, and leaned back against the sofa. "If you want to have a discussion, come over here so we can talk face to face."

Claws scraped along the rattan and then along the wood floor. Iggy climbed up on the coffee table and faced me. "I've been begging you to go to the Hex and Bones Apothecary store forever, but you never do. I've heard Mrs. Murdoch is a genius when it comes to finding the right spell. She'll know just what to do to change me back to green."

I had tried to find a solution to his problem, but perhaps I hadn't tried hard enough in Iggy's eyes. "She probably does.

Bertha Murdoch supplies all of the witches with their herbs and stuff." She also had a library of spells, but either I had convinced myself I was too busy to spend hours looking through them all, or else I feared I would mess up again. "What if I change you to some other color, like purple or blue and orange striped? You know my last few spells haven't been raging successes." More like disasters.

"Any color is better than pink. I know your track record isn't the best, but I'm willing to take the chance. I refuse to stay pink any longer." He closed his eyes in rebellion.

Iggy was being particularly anxious, and his bad vibes were beginning to rub off on me. "Why are you bringing this up now?" I held up a hand. "I realize it's on your mind a lot, but many of our town visitors come to the Tiki Hut Grill just to see a pink iguana." I loved him just the way he was.

Iggy opened his eyes and lifted his head. "Tell them to go to the Galapagos."

"You're being childish, though someday I would like to see a real pink iguana."

"A real pink iguana? What, I'm a fake?" Iggy bobbed his head.

"Watch it, buddy. Aggression is not tolerated in this household. Tell me what's really going on."

He stretched out onto his stomach and grunted. "It's bad enough that I feel useless around here, but Aimee made fun of me yesterday for being pink."

"Who the heck is Aimee?" I didn't like anyone bullying my familiar.

He looked away. "My girlfriend."

I had to work hard not to laugh, even though there was

nothing funny about romance. "You have a girlfriend?" Iggy had never mentioned he had any interest in the opposite sex.

"Yes." He lifted his head. "Do you have a problem with that?"

"Ah, no, but why haven't I heard about her before now?"

"Do you tell me about your boyfriends?"

I laughed. "What boyfriends?"

Iggy lifted a leg for a moment as if to reach for me. "Okay, your boyfriend. Singular. I know you like Sheriff Rocker."

He was trying to change the subject. "I do not like Sheriff Rocker. Okay, I don't dislike him either, but I don't have any romantic notions about him." Even if I did, I wouldn't tell blabbermouth here.

"I know you think he's hot. I overheard you talking to Penny about him."

Penny was my best girlfriend, who worked with me at the Tiki Hut Grill, and we often chatted about those things. Apparently, I wasn't aware Iggy was close enough to hear us. "I might have mentioned it once or twice. That's all." I needed to get back to Aimee. "Is your girlfriend an iguana?"

"No, she's a cat—the most beautiful black cat I've ever seen."

Ah, so that was the reason for the sudden desire to be green again. "How long have you known her?"

"A week."

A week wasn't a long time, but maybe animals were different when it came to love. "Who is her owner?"

"She doesn't have one."

I crossed my arms over my chest. "You're dating an ordinary cat?"

"No! She's special. Like me. She can talk."

Iggy was losing it. "Tell me this. Can you talk to Toto—an ordinary dog?" That was my mother's dog, who had no magical powers whatsoever. Don't worry, I know that animals communicate in different ways.

Iggy's mouth opened. "You know I can't. Toto is just a dog, but Aimee can really talk."

This was going nowhere. If Aimee could talk, then she was someone's familiar, which meant she had an owner. "Maybe you can ask her over so I can get to know her."

He shook his head. "When you invite the cute sheriff over here, I'll let you meet Aimee."

I hated when Iggy turned stubborn. "I'll tell you what. I'll go over to Hex and Bones Apothecary right now and see if there is a spell to turn a pink iguana into a green one. How does that sound?"

"Fine." He turned around, his tail swishing at me.

"What? Just fine? I thought you'd be more excited. What else is bugging you?"

He looked over his shoulder. "Like I said, I had so much fun solving Cliff's murder, and now I have nothing to do."

He hadn't actually solved the case. Many people helped bring down the killer, but ever since the case had closed, Iggy had been experiencing this feeling of emptiness. I had to admit, I was too. "You had plenty to do before you helped investigate Cliff's murder."

"Now that I have, I want more."

I sighed. "I get why you feel useless." I snapped my fingers. "Hey, I know. Why don't you apply for a job at the sheriff's department to be a detective?"

I might have been a bit sarcastic there, but it wasn't as if murders happened all that often in Witch's Cove, Florida. We were a small town on the west coast that catered to tourists. Not only did they come for our sandy beaches and endless sunshine, they enjoyed our amazing array of occult services. I have some talents in the witch department, but there weren't any that I might be paid for. For the sake of the town, that was a good thing. I couldn't tell the future or talk to the dead like my mother could.

"If Sheriff Rocker and I could communicate, that would be great, but we can't," Iggy said in his pouty voice. It wasn't attractive.

"There is that." Only witches could talk to other familiars, and Sheriff Rocker didn't qualify. Heck, he barely believed in witches or magic. "Have you ever tried to talk to him? The man could be a closet warlock." I almost laughed out loud at that thought.

"Funny, funny. We both know he's not."

"I just thought maybe I'd misjudged him." Sometimes Iggy figured things out before I did.

My familiar faced me once more and lifted the upper half of his body, looking like a sentry. "I thought you said you were going."

It was important that I show him that he was really important to me, and that I cared for his mental well-being. "I am."

I stood, shoved my credit card in my pocket and headed downstairs. Instead of leaving by the side entrance that ran through the Tiki Hut gift store, I passed through the main restaurant.

Was I being crazy for attempting this spell? Some spells I'd tried had been fairly innocuous, so if I messed up, it was no big deal. Others, however, would have had dire consequences if I'd failed—like the spell I did to find Iggy.

It was my day off from waitressing, so I had the time to ask Bertha about the ins and outs of this spell.

"Glinda, is everything okay?" Aunt Fern asked as I rushed by the checkout counter she was manning. "You look worried."

I never could fool my aunt. I stopped and backed up. After glancing around and then waving to Penny, I returned my focus to her. "Not really. Iggy is in a funk."

She set down her wand—or rather her pencil that looked like a wand. "Because he feels useless?"

"He told you?"

She tapped the side of her fairy godmother crown. "I know how hard it is when people need you, and then they don't."

Was she talking about Iggy or herself? I didn't need to get into that discussion at the moment.

"Yes, he's upset that he can no longer play detective, but he's also upset because his new girlfriend prefers him to be green instead of pink."

"Aimee?"

Really? "Is there anything you don't know?" While there was no such thing as mental telepathy—or so I believed—I wouldn't be surprised if she and Iggy communicated that way.

My aunt smiled. "I'm sure there is. Where are you headed in such a hurry?"

"I'm going to Hex and Bones Apothecary."

Aunt Fern grinned. "How exciting. Are you going to return to your witchy ways?" She wiggled her eyebrows.

I huffed out a laugh. "I have no witchy ways. Any magical abilities I possess have gone haywire too often to even call me a real witch."

"Nonsense. Bertha will not steer you wrong. Just follow her directions, and I'm sure Iggy will be green in no time."

My shoulders slumped. "For his sake, I want him to be green, but to be honest, I like him pink. It's what makes him unique."

My aunt shook her head. "You have to think what's best for him."

"I know. It's why I finally agreed to find a solution after all this time."

My aunt patted my hand. "You're doing the right thing."

"I hope so. How's Uncle Harold today, by the way?" I didn't ask often enough, but truth be told, he'd died over two years ago.

Aunt Fern claimed his ghostly body appeared most days to talk to her. I personally didn't believe in ghosts, mainly because I'd never seen one, but if she said he could communicate with her, then maybe ghosts did exist.

"He's weak. It takes energy to materialize enough for me to see him. He said he needed to rest for a few days."

My stomach cramped. "Oh, no." I couldn't ask if his condition was terminal, because he was already dead. "I probably should have asked before, but does this happen often?"

Aunt Fern tilted her head once more and smiled. When

her fairy godmother hat slipped, she righted it. "Oh, yes, but don't worry. He'll be right as rain soon."

I never did understand how rain could be right or wrong, but I let it drop. "I'll let you know how the spell for Iggy goes."

"You do that."

Contrary to popular opinion, just because she wore a fairy godmother outfit most days to work, she was not crazy. The ghost part? Maybe, but all employees—and owner as was the case with my aunt—at the Tiki Hut Grill wore a costume. The tourists loved it. I always dressed up as Glinda the Good Witch of the South, because I am a witch (albeit a fairly unsuccessful one), and I live in the south.

Aunt Fern occasionally alternated her costume, depending on her mood, but the godmother one was her favorite. I swear she chose this one because so many people spilled their deepest, darkest secrets to her just because of how she looked—sweet and trusting.

I stepped outside and immediately wilted. It was a hot June day. The silver lining was that there were enough clouds to keep me from sweating too much on the short walk to the Hex and Bones store down the road. I crossed the street and walked past the sheriff's department, working hard not to look inside. Once Steve Rocker had become the new sheriff, after Sheriff Duncan had retired—or rather had been forced to step down—I hadn't seen much of him. According to some of our second shift servers, the new sheriff usually came into the Tiki Hut for dinner, but since I had the breakfast and lunch shift, I rarely saw him.

I suppose I could have gone over to see how he was settling into the town, but I felt it would look a little suspicious. When Cliff Duncan had been murdered, Steve Rocker and I crossed paths many times—sometimes on friendly terms and at other times, not so much. While he was skeptical that I could detect how a person died, he had started to come around to my way of thinking just when he—or rather we—solved Cliff's murder.

Refocusing on the task at hand, I hurried to the apothecary shop. Once inside, I was immediately assaulted with what smelled like a combination of dust, coriander, and some other strong odor. Because the tourists expected it, there was a table with jars of bones and skulls of all shapes and sizes just inside the main entrance—all plastic knock offs, of course. Besides the usual witchy trinkets, the shop had a wall of herbs and spices, all in different sized colored containers. Each one was numbered and labeled.

Stars, moons, and ancient symbols that meant nothing to me hung by colored threads from the ceiling. Most were swaying since the air conditioner was at full blast. While some things in the store were a bit too touristy for me, the ambience of the place oozed the occult.

The catchy store's name made it ripe to sell clothing apparel with the Hex and Bones logo. Even though it was months before Halloween, the store always kept a section dedicated to dressing as a witch—or what the world thought a witch should look like. They had black hats, striped stockings, wands, and even a few black gowns. And yes, an assortment of brooms. I always got a kick out of that.

Next to that section was the candle display. I loved candles, but Bertha's were rather expensive since they were handmade. Along one side wall sat tables with ancient looking, leather bound books on them. These books contained spells and folklore. According to the owner, everything in them was authentic. It was where I might be able to find the spell to help Iggy.

"May I help you?" said a wobbly voice behind me.

I spun around, expecting to see Bertha. Instead, Hazel Silas, an ancient witch, was standing there, her shoulders hunched. I waited for her to recognize me, but when she didn't, I introduced myself. "I'm Glinda Goodall, Fern's niece." I didn't ask if she remembered me since I didn't want to embarrass her in case she didn't. We had met a few times.

"Oh, yes. You work at the Tiki Hut."

Good. She did remember. "I do." I scanned the store once more. "I'm looking for Bertha."

"I'm sorry, dear, Bertha is visiting her ill sister in Atlanta."

"That's terrible—about her sister being sick, that is. When will she be back?" I wasn't sure how long Iggy would be willing to wait.

"She doesn't know. It could be days. It could be weeks."

Decisions, decisions. If I had the ingredients in hand, it might put off Iggy for a while. "Maybe you can help me then. I need to do a spell."

Hazel's smile faltered. "Oh? What kind of spell?"

"I need to turn my pink iguana back to green."

Chapter Two

"YOU WANT TO change the color of that cute pink iguana that I've seen at the Tiki Hut to pedestrian green?"

Bright lime was hardly ordinary, but I understood her concern. "I do—or rather Iggy wants me too. He was originally green, you know, but when I conjured up my familiar many years ago, he ended up pink."

She smiled. "He's lucky to be pink."

"How so?"

"Now the two of you match." She grinned, exposing her missing two bottom teeth.

"I personally love having a distinctive pink familiar, but Iggy doesn't think so. He's getting some flak from the ladies."

Her eyes sparkled. "How nice to get paid by the ladies."

Paid? Where did she get that idea? Hazel must be hard of hearing. "No, the ladies make *fun* of him."

"No one would do that. We all think he's adorable."

Okay, this wasn't doing anyone any good. "Thank you, but Iggy wants to be normal looking again. Do you know of a spell that can help him?"

"I believe I do. I was looking through the books for another spell yesterday, and I think I saw one about returning an animal to his original form."

That was exciting. "It won't change anything but his color, right? I need for us to be able to communicate with each other." If she turned my familiar into an ordinary iguana, it would kill both of us.

"Of course, dear. Just give me a minute to locate it."

Did she even listen to what I'd just said? While Mrs. Silas searched through the books, I stepped over to the side tables. When I'd come in the last time, I'd leafed through a few. They contained love spells and curses, though it was possible there was something useful for Iggy inside of them. The tourists apparently loved these books. If I couldn't find anything, at least I would enjoy the black and white drawings.

"Oh, Glinda," Mrs. Silas called some time later. "I think I found something."

I rushed over. Not that I didn't trust Hazel Silas, but she was old, and this wasn't her store. At least I knew she was a witch. Iggy had confirmed it at one time.

"What is it?"

She flipped the large book around. Sure enough, there was the spell for returning an animal to his natural color—color that was changed because of an evil spell. I took a bit of offense with the claim that only an evil spell would change an animal. There had been nothing malicious about what I had conjured up all those years ago.

When I was twelve, my mother had dropped me off at a small grove in Hendrian National Forest several miles from town. With my spell in hand, I pictured a black cat and recited the words on the paper, careful to pronounce everything correctly. To this day, I have no idea what went wrong, but somehow a pink iguana raced down a tree and ran right up to me. When Iggy spoke, I was so happy that I didn't even consider that I'd done something wrong.

I wouldn't mess up a second time though. Determined to be even more careful this time, I read the ingredients of this spell to make sure it wasn't something crazy—like using the heart of a dragon or the eyes of an old witch. Okay, I made that up since dragons didn't exist and no, a witch would never do a spell with human eyeballs, but I didn't trust really old things.

Everything seemed to check out until I read the spell itself—or rather when I tried to read the spell. "What language is this?" I asked.

"Let me see, honey." Hazel pulled it closer and adjusted her glasses. "I have no idea, but you can read and recite, right? I don't think comprehension is a necessity for the spell to work."

Really? "What if I don't pronounce the words right?"

"Ask Miriam Daniels. She's a whiz at stuff like this."

If I had some professional guidance, it would give me more confidence. "Thanks."

Hazel checked the book once more before grabbing the many ingredients required to perform the spell. Thankfully, no one came into the store, which was a good thing since I certainly didn't need her to be distracted. She was halfway through gathering the ingredients for the potion when her cell rang.

She glanced at the screen. "Sorry, it's my sister. I need to take this."

I couldn't tell her to let it go to voicemail. It might be

important. Hazel turned her back and then reached up to take something else off the shelf. She plucked two bottles and set them on the counter, all the while conversing. Just as I was about to clear my throat, she disconnected.

"Is everything okay?" I asked.

"My sister isn't feeling well. She went to the doctors, and she's awaiting the test results. She was nervous, that's all."

Given their ages, it might be serious. "I hope she'll be okay."

"Me, too," Hazel checked the ingredients and smiled. "Good news. I have everything we need right here in the store." From below the counter, she pulled out a Bunsen Burner, a ring stand, and a beaker.

"You have to cook it?"

"Oh, yes. This is not a simple spell. It's better in its liquid form anyway. You will be drinking a half cup of it and Iggy a tablespoon. Please be sure to measure accurately."

"Why do I need to take it?"

"To boost your powers so the spell goes according to plan."

Since I didn't want to mess up anything, I was willing to try it. After all, Hazel was the expert, and I planned to do everything possible to make this work. Bertha wouldn't have put her in charge if she didn't know what she was doing. Right? "Okay."

Hazel set the beaker on the counter and carefully measured everything. Once she mixed the ingredients together, she placed the beaker on the burner and turned it on. What I didn't expect was for the liquid to turn pink. "I kind of thought it would be green since Iggy wants to be green."

Hazel looked a bit panicked, but when she looked over the instructions, she nodded. "It doesn't say what color it will be, but this will be fine."

I hoped so. "Can you copy the spell for me?" I didn't want to have come this far only to mess it up. It wasn't like I could memorize some incomprehensible words in a few minutes.

"Of course, honey. Give me a sec. I'll take this book in the office and make a copy for you."

There must be a scanner in the back. When she returned, she'd merely copied the spell by hand. I picked up the paper and tried to read it, but her shaky handwriting made it hard. "Is this an L, or an I?"

"Let me see?" Hazel adjusted her glasses and leaned over. "I think an L as in Larry."

She *thought* it was an L? "Good to know."

While I read over the spell, she let the pink potion cool before placing it in another container that she sealed. "That'll be twenty-five dollars."

For an hour's worth of her time, that was a bargain. "Are you sure that's all? You used a lot of ingredients."

"Yes. I love Iggy and want the best for him." She giggled. "From the dust on the container, I'm thinking some of these ingredients are rarely used. Bertha really needs to do a little housekeeping."

Oh, joy. I prayed the mixtures didn't lose their potency over time like some medicine did. "Thank you."

With the spell and potion in hand, I rushed out, anxious to give this a try. Before I went through with this, I had to stop at the Bubbling Cauldron Coffee Shop. Not only could I use a strong cup of coffee to calm my nerves, I had to ask for Miriam's help. The pronunciation of some of the words looked near to impossible.

As soon as Miriam spotted me near the back of her store, she smiled and waved. Coming here might have been a mistake considering she was one of the five gossip queens of Witch's Cove. Her twin sister, Maude, my Aunt Fern, Sheriff Steve Rocker's grandmother—who worked in the sheriff's office—and Dolly Andrews, the owner of the Spellbound Diner, were all prone to spread the latest gossip. I swear they lived for it. While I was worried that I might be the next headliner, I feared for Iggy's mental health more if I didn't do this spell.

Miriam came over. "This is a nice surprise, Glinda. What can I get you?"

"My usual but add an extra bit of sugar this time."

"What's wrong?" She clamped a hand over her mouth. "Don't tell me someone else died." She then waved a dismissive hand. "No, I would have heard about it if they had."

I'm sure she would have. "No one died. I'm here for your help."

Miriam loved nothing more than to be in the thick of things. "Of course, I'd love to help. Let me put in your order, and I'll be right back."

The shop was mostly empty, which meant Miriam and I could have a conversation in relative privacy. Side note: Miriam loved to tell everyone her real age, which was seventy-three, because she looked a lot younger than her twin sister, Maude, who ran the tea shop across the street. Maude had been ill a few years back and hadn't aged well as a result.

Miriam pulled up a chair. "What can I do for you?"

I showed her the spell and explained how I was going to attempt to change Iggy's color from pink to green. "I want to make certain I can pronounce these words correctly."

"Let me look." She read over the six lines of the spell. "I can help you. Read it to me first, and I'll see if you pronounce any words wrong."

I did as she asked. The more I read, the more her lips pressed together. I wouldn't have minded, but the sighing was a bit unsettling. I finished and put down the paper. "That bad?"

"No, not at all. With a little practice, your spell will be perfect."

Her assistant delivered the coffee. I blew on the surface to cool it before taking a sip. It was delicious, as usual. "Just what I needed."

Miriam waited patiently. "Try again."

Since spells didn't need to be read quickly, I recited the words slowly, enunciating everything clearly. When I finished, I held my breath. "How was that?"

She grinned. "Perfect, but I will miss seeing Iggy's pink little body wiggling around the Tiki Hut."

"Me, too." I snapped my fingers. "I forgot to ask Hazel if I needed to light any candles or have incense when I did the spell."

"Hazel?"

Uh-oh. "Yes, Hazel Silas. Bertha is away visiting her sister."

"I knew that, but I wasn't aware she'd asked Hazel to take

over."

Suddenly, the coffee soured in my stomach. "Do you think she doesn't know what she's doing?"

Miriam waved. "She's fine. Hazel can read. As long as she isn't required to substitute any ingredients, you have nothing to worry about."

I breathed a sigh of relief. "She claimed she had everything in the store. I'm more worried about me messing up. My spells haven't been all that successful in the past."

"I hear Gertrude Poole is giving classes in spells."

"I didn't know that. I will look into it. But what about candles and stuff for this spell? Should I go back and ask her what I need?" I had seen a few spell books that listed what was required—like candles and spices—in order to complete the spell. When my mother did her seances, she used those things.

Miriam's lip twisted to the side. "I wouldn't bother asking. I don't think either could hurt if you add them. Like I always tell my sister, better to be safe than sorry."

I had candles. I had incense. I also had some dried sage at the house. I was good to go. "Okay. I'll do it all."

Since I didn't need Miriam's help anymore, she left to attend to her store. I mentally went over what I had to do, and I believed I was as prepared as I'd ever be. For Iggy's sake, I wanted this to work.

After I paid, I crossed the street and headed to the Tiki Hut. Not wanting to be grilled by Aunt Fern until I'd tried the spell, I entered through the side door. At the base of the stairs that led to my upstairs apartment, I inhaled. I could do this.

When I went inside my place though, I nearly stepped on

Iggy. "Hey, be careful. I almost tripped over you."

"Did you get it?"

"Yes, I have the potion. Give me a sec to put down my stuff."

He hopped on top of the coffee table, his mouth open and his tail moving rapidly from side to side. "How does this work?"

"I light a few candles and some incense, spread some herbs around, and say the spell."

"How many candles? Too many, and the spirits might be blinded. Light too few and they'll think you aren't serious."

I chuckled. "There was no mention that I even needed them. I thought it might get us in the mood if we have candles and incense."

His eyes closed for a moment. He then bobbed his head and opened his eyes. "I agree."

Good. "First, I need a measuring cup and a tablespoon. We each have to drink some of the potion."

"We have to drink it? I'm not sure I want to. What if it makes me sick?"

"I have to drink it too. Are you having second thoughts?"

He lifted his head. "No."

"Good." I went into the kitchen and retrieved what I needed.

Once back in the living room, I put down the pink potion, along with the measuring cup and tablespoon. I located the candles and incense sticks and lit them. I then gathered the herbs. With everything all set, I finally sat down. "Ready?" I asked him.

Chapter Three

IGGY NODDED HIS assent. I still couldn't believe I'd agreed to this crazy spell. I took out the paper with the magic words on it. "First, we drink, and then I say the words."

"How long will it take before I turn green?" Iggy asked.

"I don't know. It will take as long as it takes."

"That's not an answer." He was getting huffy again.

"It's the best I can do. Hazel didn't give me a time frame."

"Hazel? As in Hazel Silas?"

My heart nearly stopped again. "Yes, why?"

"What happened to Bertha?"

I told him about her sick sister. "It will be okay. I had Miriam go over the spell with me."

"Hazel is pretty old. I think her eyesight is bad. I don't trust her."

He was just nervous. "Don't worry. It'll be fine. We can do this." Or were those merely famous last words?

Not wanting to waste any more time, I chugged the pink potion, not sure what to expect. To my surprise, the taste was actually pleasant. It was a cross between peppermint candy and Pepto Bismol. Iggy waited a beat, probably to see if I would keel over. When I didn't seem to have any adverse reaction, he lapped up the liquid.

With the drinking portion complete, I slowly read the spell out loud, thankful Iggy didn't interrupt me. He was probably chomping at the bit to complain the words weren't in English. A few of them sounded somewhat familiar though. If I had to hazard a guess, I'd say it was either very old English or some kind of Gaelic dialogue.

I put down the paper and waited. Iggy didn't move or blink. He just stared at me. Even the air was still. It was almost as if the world was waiting for the change. He lifted a leg, looked down, and wiggled his toes. At least the spell hadn't harmed him physically.

"How do you feel?" I asked. I was more interested to know if he could still communicate with me.

"The same. You?"

"The same." Thank goodness, he could talk. I picked up the paper again and reread it, wondering what had gone wrong.

"You have no idea how long this will take?"

He'd already asked me that. "No. Be patient."

I was trying to be upbeat, but in truth, I was devastated—for Iggy's sake. He desperately wanted this.

Ten minutes later, my patience had run out. "I'm fixing some tea. Do you want a sip of water or some arugula?" It was Iggy's favorite food—besides hibiscus flowers.

"No." He hopped down from the coffee table and crawled over to his stool of safety. Waves of disappointment washed off him.

I was tempted to go back to Hazel and have her call Bertha, but what good would that do? The spell was done. It didn't work. The end.

I fixed my tea and made a plate of greens for Iggy. Eventually, he'd eat it. Unless he decided to go on a hunger strike just to show his disappointment. When I returned to the living room, he was gone. "Iggy?"

Claw marks scraping against the wooden floor sounded in the hallway. As tempted as I was to try to make him feel better, I let him go. He was probably going to either chat with Aunt Fern or seek solace with Aimee. Both might be better company than me right now.

I polished off my tea and set the arugula leaves on Iggy's empty stool. It was time to tell Aunt Fern that I failed—again. I headed downstairs, half expecting Iggy to be perched on the counter top, but he wasn't there. My aunt was chatting with a customer at the checkout counter. When they spotted me, the man smiled and then excused himself. He seemed happy for the excuse to get away. I understood. Aunt Fern could talk the ear off of anyone.

"How did it go?" Aunt Fern's eyes sparkled.

"It didn't go. Iggy left in a huff. I thought he might be down here."

"If he is, I didn't see him."

"He probably left through the back entrance," I said.

"What do you think went wrong?" my aunt asked.

"I have no idea." And that depressed me more than anything. "If my ability to communicate with Iggy wasn't intact, I might not believe I'm a witch at all."

Aunt Fern patted my hand. "Nonsense. That magic necklace of yours still works."

I ran my fingers across the surface of the pink diamond pendant, or rather the fake pink diamond pendant. My grandmother had given it to me, and considering she wasn't well off, it probably wasn't real. I still believed I could tell how a person had died. "There's that."

My aunt pulled the bank's money pouch from under the counter. "Would you do me a favor? It will save me a trip."

"Sure."

"Deposit this in the bank."

Getting out for a walk would do me good, and she probably understood that. "I'd be happy to."

I took the pouch and headed back upstairs for my backpack purse. Not that there was much crime in this town, but I didn't want to advertise I was carrying a wad of cash. Once I packed up, I left.

The bank sat behind the large parking lot that was across the street. I headed south one block. As soon as I crossed the street, a cold chill brushed my arm. I slowed, curious what that was.

"You could at least say excuse me." The deep male voice behind me sounded far off and rather strained.

I whipped around but saw no one. "Hello?"

My pulse soared at the possibility that the weakened voice came from someone who was injured—only I didn't see him. No one else was nearby, so I waited a minute before deciding that I must have been imagining things. I spun back around and nearly ran into someone—or at least I thought it was a someone.

The man was pale—and kind of wavy, if that was even possible. It must have been the sunlight shining in my eyes because he seemed to be a bit translucent.

"You can see me?" he asked with an incredible amount of

surprise.

"I guess, though you don't look well."

"To be honest, I'm not doing all that well."

He turned his back to me, and I gasped. A large red blood stain ran from shoulder to shoulder. "Oh, my goodness, you're injured. I'll call 911."

He faced me. "Don't bother."

Don't bother? "Why not?"

"I'm dead."

That was an expression I used quite often. Actually, I thought I might be dead to Iggy since I had just failed him. "You aren't dead."

To be sure I wasn't crazy, I reached out to touch him but felt nothing solid—only another blast of cold air. Dread pooled in my stomach at what this might mean. "What's your name?" I asked, failing to keep the shake out of my voice.

"Morgan Oliver, and I need your help."

If he wasn't solid, he had to be dead, right? Or was he some hologram, and this was some joke on me? "How can I help if you're deceased?"

I looked around to see who else was nearby. I wanted confirmation that I wasn't crazy. Surely, I couldn't be standing in front of a gh…ghost! That would be insane. Ghosts didn't exist anymore than werewolves or vampires did.

He placed his hand over his heart, but the tips of his fingers dug into his body. He then lowered his hand. "I won't have any peace until I find out who shot me."

"You don't know?"

"No. Someone shot me in the back!"

"Okay, okay. Calm down. Are you from Witch's Cove?"

"No, but my uncle lives here—or at least he did. He died. He recently told me he'd written me into his will to inherit his farm."

"Who's your uncle?" Was it Floyd Paxton, the man a wolf had attacked a few weeks ago?

Before he told me, Morgan disappeared—as in evaporated.

"Glinda?" said a voice I knew too well. I spun around.

"Sheriff Rocker. Nice to see you." I was tempted for a moment to reach out and touch him to make sure he was solid and not some ghost, but he looked quite alive.

"Are you okay?" he asked.

"Why wouldn't I be?" I worked to put as much calm into my voice as possible.

"Ah, because you've been standing in the parking lot for the last minute talking to yourself," he said.

He'd been watching me? Morgan Oliver reappeared—if you could call semi-transparent appearing—next to the sheriff, but now the sparkle in the ghost's eyes was gone.

"Don't worry," the ghost said. "He can't see me."

Don't worry? Every muscle in my body was frozen. I'd really just met a ghost. As if Morgan understood his time was up, he faded away.

The sheriff reached out and cupped my shoulder. Clearly, he thought I needed help. Hey, maybe I did. I had to come up with an answer that wouldn't make him commit me to a psychiatric hospital. "I was practicing what I wanted to tell my mom. My father hasn't been feeling well, and she won't tell me why." My face heated at the half lie.

"I'm sorry to hear about your dad. Why don't you come

next door to the Bubbling Cauldron, and I'll buy you a coffee? You look like you could use one."

"I'm okay. I promised Aunt Fern I'd take the day's receipts to the bank." I reached behind me and patted the lower part of my pack.

"Are you sure?" he asked.

As much as I wanted to ask him about Morgan Oliver, I needed time to process what happened. "I'm sure. Maybe another time."

"Of course. Just let me know."

Embarrassed by that encounter, I hightailed it out of there. After I deposited the daily receipts in the bank, I decided to have a little chat with Hazel. Maybe she could shed some light on my dilemma.

Inside the Hex and Bones Apothecary, Hazel was with a young woman I'd never seen before. That meant either the person was a tourist or didn't eat at the Tiki Hut Grill. While Hazel took care of her, I returned to the stack of spell books along the side wall. I wasn't sure what I was looking for, but I thought there might be something about ghost sightings in one of them.

I was engrossed in the drawings when someone tapped me on the shoulder. I jumped. Thank goodness, it was only Hazel—and not Morgan Oliver. I honestly didn't even know if he touched me whether or not I'd feel it. Even though my aunt could see ghosts—or rather at least one ghost—I wasn't up to speed on their habits or abilities.

Hazel was slightly bent over, and she wasn't meeting my gaze at first. "Glinda. I'm happy you came back. I am so sorry."

My pulse soared. "About what?"

"It was only after you left that I realized when I was on the phone with my sister that I pulled down the wrong ingredient, which means the spell to change Iggy won't work."

I had to take a moment to wrap my brain around what happened. On the one hand, I was upset that Hazel had messed up. On the other, that meant it hadn't been my fault. "That's okay. How about mixing me another batch, and I'll give it another go?"

She sucked in a breath. "I'm afraid it doesn't work that way. The two key ingredients, when combined, can only be used once in a person's lifetime. I was so distraught over my mistake that I called Bertha to ask her how to remedy this. She said what was done was done."

I'd never heard of only being able to ingest ingredients one time. Iggy would be devastated, but at least I hadn't been the one to make the mistake. "I'll let Iggy down gently." Here came the hard part. I glanced around to make sure no one else had come in. "By drinking that particular pink potion, do you think there might be any side effects?"

Hazel's face paled, and then she pressed her lips together. "Maybe. Are you having *hallucinations*, by any chance?"

I heaved a sigh. "Yes. A hallucination." I actually laughed. "And here I thought I saw a ghost! Phew. That is a relief."

I expected her to smile and pat my arm. Instead, she pulled out a chair next to me and sat down. "We need to talk."

Uh-oh. That didn't sound good. I leaned closer. "Don't tell me I really did see a ghost."

"I'm afraid so."

I needed to put a positive spin on this. "It's a one-time event, right? It's not like I'm going to see everyone who ever died walking the streets, am I?"

The color finally returned to Hazel's face. "Absolutely not. Most people only see one ghost, and that's it."

I wasn't sure if I should mention Morgan's request, but Hazel appeared to be very open-minded. "I met a man by the name of Morgan Oliver." I waited a beat to see if she'd seen or heard of him. When she said nothing, I continued. "He was murdered, though I don't know how long ago."

Logic told me that if his uncle had died recently and left the farm to Morgan, the ghost would have been murdered after that. That meant there would be a record of Morgan Oliver's death. Or was my brain a bit fried from the potion?

"I've never heard of him. Maybe the sheriff can do a search."

I actually laughed. "How can I ask about a dead guy? The sheriff would never believe me if I said I spoke with a ghost."

Hazel rubbed the forefinger and thumb of her right hand together and looked over my head. It must be her way of thinking. "Say, you're related to him or something, and that you want to locate him. I wouldn't mention that he's dead."

I had to hand it to her. That wasn't a bad idea. "I might do that."

As soon as I stood, she clasped my hand. "Please tell Iggy that I'm sorry."

"I will." As I pushed back my chair, I bumped into something—something that meowed loudly. I whipped around. "I'm sorry, kitty. I didn't mean to hit you."

"Be careful the next time," the cat said, loud and clear.

My heart nearly stopped. The cat could talk! Not that my familiar wasn't a chatterbox, but at least he wore a collar when he went sightseeing. This one looked a bit ragged—as in this animal lived on the streets. This was the second time today that I'd heard about a talking black cat. Maybe there was a family of them.

Hazel leaned over and petted the kitty. "You want something to drink, Aimee?"

Aimee? Could she be Iggy's girlfriend? "She's your familiar?" I asked.

Hazel slumped back in the chair. "No. I mean maybe, kind of. I did name her."

The old witch wasn't making any sense. "Either she is your familiar or she isn't. Iggy's girlfriend is also named Aimee."

"He said that?" Aimee asked. Her tone was a mixture of excitement and anger, if that was even possible.

"Yes."

As much as I wanted to chat with her, I needed to find out how this cat was able to talk if she wasn't Hazel's familiar. Or did she belong to someone else? I leaned over. "Iggy said you've been in town a week. Is that true?"

"Yes and no," Aimee said. She lifted her head and nodded to Hazel. "I've only been able to talk for about a week. That's what I meant. You need to ask the witch here what happened."

Ouch. That wasn't nice. "You don't know?"

"Not completely," Aimee said.

"How do you think it happened? I want to hear your side."

Her back arched for a second. "Fine. I've lived on the street for the last few years. I was looking for something to eat when I wandered in here. That's when *she* changed me."

"How?"

"How should I know?"

Testy little animal. I needed answers, so I turned back to Hazel. "What can you tell me about it?"

Hazel sighed. "Aimee's right. It's all my fault. A young girl had come into the shop needing the ingredients for the spell to get her familiar from the forest."

"I did that many, many years ago," I said.

"I know. This girl was really nervous. She wanted me to read the spell to her to make sure she didn't mess it up."

That sounded familiar. "Even if you'd held the potion in your hand and read the spell, that wouldn't have turned an ordinary cat into a talking one," I said.

Aimee rubbed her head against my legs. I looked down at her. "Is that how you remember it?"

"Not exactly," the cat said with way too much sass.

"Hazel, please tell me."

She exhaled deeply. "I honestly didn't know Aimee was in the store. When she bumped into me, I was so startled that I knocked over the jar that had the potion in it. The lid must not have been on very well, because it fell on the cat."

"And gave me a bump on my head. Do you know how much glass hurts when it falls?"

My heart went out to the cat. I looked back at Hazel. "Why do you think Aimee isn't your familiar?"

"Because the spell wasn't said in the woods." She huffed an exasperated breath. "I can't really explain it, but the potion and the reciting of the spell must have triggered something inside of her."

Aimee meowed. "It took a few days for me to calm down, but now I think it's cool that I can talk, though the first time Iggy spoke back to me, I freaked."

"I can only imagine. If you want, you can come back with me to the apartment. I'm sure Iggy would be happy to see you."

Aimee hesitated. "Okay, but I don't believe in cohabitation." I tried not to laugh. "We're only friends. I'll go with you and say hi, but then I'm out of there."

Out of there? That wasn't very hospitable. Aimee's attitude left something to be desired, but if Iggy liked her, that was all that mattered. "Just so you know, he's really depressed right now because the spell to change him back to green failed. Seeing you will help."

"I hope so. He seems kind of nice."

Only kind of nice?

Hazel pushed back her chair and stood. "Again, I'm sorry. I can't wait until Bertha returns. This spell stuff is stressing me out."

It stressed me out too. "I can understand why."

With Aimee behind me, I headed out. I honestly expected her to run away, but thankfully, she didn't. When we reached the Tiki Hut Grill, instead of going through the restaurant and having my aunt question me, I went through the side entrance once more.

I was halfway up the stairs when a sound behind me made me look over my shoulder. I had to blink a few times to make sure I wasn't seeing things. "Uncle Harold?"

Chapter Four

THE TRANSPARENT FIGURE wavered a bit and then looked almost solid. "Glinda, you can see me?"

"Yes." At least I thought I was looking at my uncle's ghost. I needed Aunt Fern to confirm it though. "Can you ask your wife to come here?" I asked as sweetly as possible.

He smiled. "Sure."

My heart pounded as he disappeared. A moment later, my aunt rushed back in. "Harold told me you can see him. Is that true?"

I had to grab the handrail to steady myself. "Yes. I thought I might be imagining things." That would be two ghosts in one day!

She planted a hand on her chest, and her breaths came out so fast I thought she might hyperventilate. I rushed down the stairs to make sure she didn't pass out—right after I regained my balance.

"What's going on?" Aimee asked as she followed me back down the stairs.

"Not now, Aimee. Go see Iggy. He's up the stairs on the right. There's a cat door." I didn't want to deal with her as well as Uncle Harold. All of this magic coming at me at once was overwhelming me.

"Did that black cat just talk, or am I imagining things?" my aunt asked.

"The cat can talk. It's a long story."

My aunt clenched and unclenched her fists. "You go upstairs. I'm going to find someone to take over the cash register. Then I'll be right up, Glinda. We need to have a chat." She turned to her dead husband. "Come on, Harold. You have some explaining to do."

Aunt Fern turned around and rushed back down the hall with Harold trailing after her. My head wouldn't stop spinning. I was in enough shock that I'd talked to a ghost by the name of Morgan Oliver, but to see Uncle Harold again really made me question my sanity. At the moment, I thought maybe both Aunt Fern and I had lost it.

Some howling sounded in my apartment, and I rushed upstairs to see what was going on. I had assumed Iggy would be thrilled to see Aimee, but someone wasn't happy.

When I opened the door, Iggy was on his perch facing the window, and Aimee was circling the sofa. "What happened?" I asked.

"You invited her here?" Iggy asked, not facing me.

"Kind of. Yes. I thought you'd be thrilled."

"Is Aimee going to live here?" he asked, his head bobbing.

Where was this coming from? "I merely asked if she wanted to visit you."

Iggy turned around. "You're not replacing me then?"

That was the last thing I expected him to say. "Iggy, no. You are my familiar and always will be. Aimee happened to be in the right spot at the right time to receive the gift of speech. I'm sure she told you what happened, but she is never going to *be* you."

"That's right, Iggy. You're this woman's familiar, not me. Since you don't want me here, I'm leaving," she said.

"Don't leave, Aimee," I said, sounding way too stressed. "Iggy is just in one of his moods."

She faced me and then sat down, her tail whipping back and forth across the wooden floor. "I don't stay where I'm not welcome. Thanks for inviting me though. And just so you know, I never said that I wanted Iggy to be green. He made that up."

I turned back to him. "Is that true?"

He scratched his face, clearly stalling. "Maybe."

"Why did you tell me Aimee made fun of you?"

"I know how much you hate bullies. I thought it might light a fire under you to get that spell."

What a manipulative jerk. "We will discuss your lie later."

Aimee rose onto all fours and trotted over to Iggy, her head held high. "If you want to talk, you know where to find me, but never use me as an excuse. Ever again. Do you hear me?"

"Loud and clear," Iggy said, not making eye contact.

With that she slipped out of the cat door. I guess my days as a matchmaker were over. I walked over to Iggy. "Why were you rude to her? And why did you say Aimee wanted to change you?"

"I figured if I looked normal, she'd really like me."

Poor Iggy. "She'll like you if you are yourself."

"Maybe. Did you find out what happened with the spell?"

"Yes." I explained about the mix up in ingredients and how we weren't able to try again. "It was when I was learning about it from Hazel that I met Aimee."

"Are you saying I'll always be pink?"

"I'm afraid so."

"Then I need some space."

I figured as much. "I understand," I said. "Besides, I have some other issues to deal with right now."

"Like what?" His interest was sparked.

"I saw Uncle Harold."

That ought to catch his attention. Iggy spun around so fast his collar almost came off. "You saw a ghost?"

Someone knocked at the door, and before I had the chance to answer, Aunt Fern stepped inside. I looked behind her for Uncle Harold, but he wasn't there. "Where is he?" I asked.

"In his desire for you to see him, he used up a lot of energy. He's lying down—or doing whatever he does to rest. You can see him later." Aunt Fern went over to the sofa, sat down, and patted the seat next to her. "Come and sit. Tell me what happened. You've never been able to see a ghost before."

Iggy scurried over to the coffee table and climbed up for a front row seat.

I went through the whole thing about how and why the pink potion went wrong. "Hazel feels badly about it. What's worse is that she said the spell to change Iggy's color back to green won't work a second time for some reason."

He opened and then closed his mouth—his version of a shrug. "At least Aimee understands how spells can go wrong."

"Yes, especially since she was the recipient of a bad one," I said. "Or a good one, depending on her perspective."

Aunt Fern reached out and placed a palm on my arm. "I

don't understand how you can see Harold though. What changed?"

I explained how one side effect of the combination of ingredients Hazel used was that I could see ghosts. "The first time I saw one was when I was on the street next to the Bubbling Cauldron Coffee shop."

"You've seen two ghosts today?" my aunt asked.

"Yes." I detailed my short interaction with Morgan Oliver.

Iggy spun around. "We get to solve another murder!"

His excitement buoyed my spirits. "I know his name, but I don't know where Morgan is from or when he died."

"We know that farmer. What's his name, the one who died a few weeks ago?" Iggy asked. He sure was quick to pick up the other unsolved crime. "It sounds like this Morgan guy died after that."

"Do you mean Floyd Paxton—the farmer who lived on the edge of town?" I asked.

"Yes, yes. That's it! You need to see if Morgan, the ghost, is his nephew," Iggy said, wearing his imaginary detective hat.

I held up a hand. "Okay. I'll see if I can find out if Floyd had any sisters. If he didn't, then Morgan Oliver would have been related on Floyd's wife's side."

"As much as I hate to suggest it," Aunt Fern said, "Dolly Andrews is really into genealogy. She'd know how to find out about his family."

A bit of calm surrounded me. "Thank you. I might ask her, but first I'll search the newspaper for Floyd's obituary. That usually lists next of kin. If Morgan Oliver was related to Floyd, he might have been the one to provide the information."

"Well, Emma didn't," her aunt said.

"Emma?"

"Floyd's wife. If you ask Miriam, or maybe it was Maude Daniels, they'll say Floyd killed her since no one has seen her for months. Personally, I think she ran away."

There was only one real reason for her to do that. "Did he hit her or something?"

"Rumor has it that he did and more than once."

Abuse was so sad. "Even though a wolf, or wolves, killed Floyd, I wonder if either Sheriff Duncan or Deputy Rocker were able to contact his wife to tell her of his death. She should know it is safe to return home."

Aunt Fern smiled. "That's an excellent question. You should go talk to him."

I knew that look. "My visit would be strictly for information, not to flirt."

"Uh-huh."

My aunt was incorrigible.

"I want to come," Iggy said.

I didn't want to disappoint him, but now wasn't the time. "Maybe on my next trip."

"You're no fun."

Aunt Fern stood. "I need to check on Harold. Let me know what you find out."

"I will." I stood and hugged her. "I'll chat with Uncle Harold later. We have a lot to catch up on." I didn't dare ask if Harold *slept* in one spot or if he floated around all day. Aunt Fern and I never discussed those kind of details, mostly because I didn't believe in ghosts—or at least never had before. Oh, how one day could change my view on life.

"He'd love that. I know he gets a little bored talking to me all the time."

Once my aunt left, I fished out my laptop and searched for Floyd Paxton's obituary. No surprise, Iggy was perched next to me, totally excited about our potential new adventure.

"There," he said, as I scrolled the online Obit section of the newspaper.

"I see it. It says that Floyd Paxton was survived by his wife, Emma Oliver Paxton, and his brother Charles. It doesn't mention anyone else, but at least we can conclude that Morgan comes from Floyd's wife's side of the family since her maiden name was Oliver."

Iggy hopped on my lap, probably to get a closer view. "It doesn't say where Charles lives," he said.

"No, but I'll type in Morgan Oliver's name into the computer and see what comes up."

Iggy swished his tail. "This is like old times."

I looked at him. "We've solved one crime. That doesn't make us amateur detectives, you know."

"Sure it does."

I didn't need to be arguing with him. After setting him back down onto the sofa cushion, I did a ZabaSearch on the Internet and found Morgan Oliver's name. The address was from Liberty, Florida, which was about a thirty-minute drive from here. "He lived in Liberty," I told Iggy.

"Let's go," Iggy said.

"Go where?"

"To Morgan's hometown. I bet the sheriff there will know what happened to him. He must have a list of suspects a mile long."

"That's true, but the department won't tell me any details. Morgan's murder is still unsolved, or so he seems to think." I snapped my fingers. "Steve could find out though."

"Good thinking."

Before I left to pick the sheriff's brain, I searched for open murder cases in Liberty, together with Morgan's name. Sure enough, there were a few articles about his death, but no one had been arrested. This confirmed—at least to me—that I had really seen a ghost.

"What are you going to ask hunky Steve?" Iggy asked.

"That's Sheriff Rocker or Sheriff Steve to you. Be respectful."

Iggy stuck his tongue out at me. "I promise not to call him that to his face."

My familiar knew that Steve couldn't hear him anyway. "Thank you. Since my ghost lived close to here, I can't tell Steve he was a lost relative. I'll have to come up with something plausible."

"Do you know if Morgan Oliver was married?" Iggy asked.

"No, but I'm not saying he's my ex-husband if that's what you're thinking."

"It was worth a shot."

Iggy was crazy. "I have his address. I'll talk to a few neighbors to see what they know."

"That could be dangerous." Iggy wasn't often this protective, but I was pleased to know he cared.

"It could be, but if the killer murdered Morgan, he probably got what he wanted—whatever that was. But don't worry. I'm not a too-stupid-to-live person who hears a noise at night and then goes downstairs to investigate. Nope. Not me. I am careful."

"Sure, you are," Iggy said.

"Fine. It might be dangerous, but I can't ask the sheriff to investigate. Liberty isn't part of his jurisdiction. Besides, he'll want to know why I have a sudden interest in this case."

"Tell him the truth. What harm can it do? He already thinks you're a little *strange*."

Sadly, that was true. "Okay, I'll give it a try, but you're still not coming with me." There was only so much *strange* a person could handle at one time.

"Fine. I'll find Aimee and try to smooth things out between us."

"I think that's an excellent idea. You do realize that lying about what Aimee said is totally unacceptable, don't you? Women like honesty."

Iggy lifted his head. "I'll keep that in mind."

I grabbed my keys and phone, locked the front door, and left. Aunt Fern was downstairs, but since she was cashing someone out, I waved and then scurried out. Being the ever-curious person that she was, I expected her to watch me cross the street and then enter the sheriff's office.

When I stepped inside the building, I smelled the wonderful scent of chocolate chip cookies right before I spotted a pile of them on a plate on the receptionist's desk. I was surprised Pearl hadn't ingested them all by now. She loved her sweets.

"Glinda. Here to get your ticket punched?" Pearl asked with a smile.

"Excuse me?"

She laughed. "Don't you remember the last time you were here I said that if you visit nine times, you get a cookie on the tenth visit?"

"I do, but I thought you were kidding." Though how embarrassing was it that Steve's grandmother was actually keeping track of how often I showed up? I had come quite often during the former deputy's murder investigation.

"What can we do for you today?" Pearl asked, her face rather animated.

"I'd like to speak with the sheriff. It's about a murder."

Pearl's lined face paled. "A murder? Who? When?"

I'd stepped in it now. I waved a hand. "It's an old case that has caught my interest. I thought Steve—I mean Sheriff Rocker—might have heard of it. It happened over in Liberty." I didn't want to be forced to tell her about my ghost sighting. If I could figure out a way to learn about Morgan's death without revealing that I was a weirdo, I would, but I also didn't want to lie. I needed Steve Rocker on my side.

"Let me buzz my grandson."

It wasn't as if he was in another office. He was at his old deputy desk about fifteen feet behind her. Pearl called him, and he picked up right away. As he spoke to his grandmother, he swiveled his desk chair and faced us. It was interesting that he hadn't moved into the sheriff's office. Maybe he was waiting until he had a deputy.

Once he hung up, Steve smiled and waved me over. I was pretty sure that as soon as I told him what I saw, he'd never see me in the same way again.

"Glinda."

"Sheriff, I have a dilemma." I didn't want to dance around the truth.

He motioned I take a seat. "What can I help you with today? Did you find out someone didn't die like they were supposed to?"

That might have happened a time or two before. Just not today. "This is not about a dead body. At least not in the way you think."

He leaned back in his chair and twirled the pencil that had been in his hand. I so wanted to wipe the amused look off his face. I didn't know what it would take for him to believe I had powers.

"Talk to me. I have the time. Witch's Cove has been rather calm since Cliff's death. Not even a robbery—except for the one at Floyd Paxton's place."

"Funny you should mention that. Do you have any leads as to who robbed him?"

His cheer disappeared. "No. Considering Floyd's house was such a mess, it would take ten years to dust everything for prints. There was nothing on the front door knob, other than the deceased's prints. Why? Do you know something?"

"Not exactly. What about his wife? Did you ever locate her? Maybe she has an idea what was taken."

He studied me for a few seconds, probably trying to decide whether to tell me anything. "We've not been able to find her."

"If you can believe one of the Daniels sisters, Floyd killed his wife and buried her on his property."

The sheriff froze. "That is a rather gruesome thought. Considering Floyd's farm spans over a hundred acres, I doubt we'd find her even if we looked. Not only that, we don't have the manpower to do such a large search. At the moment, I'm the only one on the force."

"Do you plan to hire a deputy?"

"Yes, as soon as we find someone suitable. It's in the mayor's hands right now."

I crossed my legs, pretending to look relaxed. "Good to know. You said that wolves killed Floyd. Do you still think that's true?"

"Yes. Why wouldn't I? The medical examiner confirmed it was an animal attack."

"I see. Well, if Emma Paxton is alive, I imagine she stands to inherit the farm. I would think she'd come back at some point." I wasn't ready to discuss Morgan just yet.

"I agree, assuming she's learned her husband has died. But the problem is that Floyd's nephew on his wife's side was the beneficiary—not her. We looked into it." Steve twisted toward his computer and tapped a few keys. "We scanned the will. The nephew is Morgan Oliver. He inherited the land and the house. Not Emma."

Problem solved. I wasn't sure if I should mention that Morgan was dead and that I'd spoken with him. "Did you question him? Maybe Morgan Oliver trashed the place. He could have been looking for the will."

Steve's eyes widened. "He might have, but why are you interested? Floyd Paxton wasn't murdered, or do you like to snoop in every legal case?"

What seemed clear, was that Steve thought I was trying to step on his toes. "No, I don't, but I've met Morgan Oliver."

His brows rose. "Is that so? When?"

"Today."

He laughed. "You have the wrong guy then, because the sheriff over in Liberty told me Morgan Oliver was murdered last week. She let me know as a courtesy since he stood to inherit the farm in our county, which now, obviously, he won't."

The sheriff was a woman? It would make sense for them to join forces. "Does *she* know who killed him?"

"I didn't ask. If Morgan Oliver was the one to ransack Floyd's house, then it's not like he can be prosecuted now, can he?" the sheriff said.

This wasn't going as planned. "Okay, because I need your help, I have to come right out and tell you the truth."

His eyebrows rose. "Please do. I need some entertainment today."

I was tempted to leave, but I'd promised Morgan that I'd help him. The question was where to begin. Discussing Iggy and his desire to change back to green would give Steve a reason to commit me. "Do you remember this morning when you saw me talking to myself?"

"Yes. You were practicing a speech to deliver to your mom."

"That was what I said, but that wasn't true." And here I had just preached to Iggy about always telling the truth. I was such a hypocrite.

"I figured."

Then why did he pretend as if he believed me? It didn't matter. I inhaled. "Here goes."

Chapter Five

"I WAS TALKING to a ghost—Morgan Oliver's ghost to be exact," I said.

I couldn't believe how hard my heart was beating. It wasn't until that moment that I realized I cared what Steve thought of me. I should have gone to Drake first. My best male friend understood about Iggy and magic potions. He wouldn't have laughed, like Steve Rocker was trying hard not to do.

"You spoke to a ghost? Hmm. I find that fascinating." His lips twitched upward.

"I'm serious," I said.

"I am too. Tell me more."

He didn't believe me. If I didn't need his information, I would have left. "The short of it was that I was trying to do a spell—for what or for whom doesn't matter. The point is that it went wrong. Really wrong, and I ended up being able to see ghosts. Believe me when I say that until today, I absolutely didn't believe in them—at all! It didn't matter that Aunt Fern claims she can see her dead husband. Uncle Harold apparently talks to her every day, but I thought it was all in her head."

"Hmm. Talking to ghosts is a little out there."

"I agree. I wouldn't believe me either, but the fact remains, I saw one and had a conversation with Morgan Oliver. Because he was a bit transparent, I believed I either walked right through him the first time or brushed against him. That means he was definitely a ghost."

"I need to do a little research, but how did you know it was him?"

"He told me his name and then said that he'd been murdered." From the way Steve's eyes had changed to a darker color, he didn't believe me. Or was the light changing in the room?

"Your ghost was transparent?" Steve asked.

That's what he got out of my comment? "Yes. As in, I could almost see through him, but not quite. For a ghost to be seen, he has to use a lot of energy—or so he said. As it was, Morgan was only visible for maybe two minutes, but he showed me the bullet hole in his back—or rather I saw the back of his bloodstained shirt."

Steve pressed his lips together and then withdrew a yellow pad of paper from his desk drawer. "What was your ghost wearing?" This time his tone was quite professional.

"Uh…I didn't pay all that much attention. I was kind of in shock talking to a dead person."

"Could you tell how old he was?" Steve asked.

I searched my memory. "Maybe thirty, thirty-five. I mean, he was dead. Morgan's skin was a bit pale. That kind of thing can really age a person."

"Uh-huh." Steve scribbled down the information. "What else did he say?"

"Not much. Just that his uncle had recently died and left the farm to him."

"Did he mention that his uncle was Floyd Paxton?" Steve asked.

"No. He disappeared before he could give me a name. I think it was just about the time you showed up."

"Of course. I must have scared him off." Steve took notes. "You don't remember anything about what he was wearing?"

I closed my eyes for a moment. "Jeans and a white T-shirt, though the back was plastered in blood."

"Where was the wound located, exactly?" he asked.

I didn't see the purpose of this, but I opened my eyes and told him anyway. "Between the shoulder blades."

More scribbling. "I'll tell you what I'll do. I'll contact Misty over in Liberty and see what she has to say. The death of Morgan Oliver is her case."

He really called her Misty? Not Sheriff Whatever? "Thank you."

And no, I'm not jealous one bit.

While he didn't promise he'd let me know what he found, I'm sure I'd learn about it one way or the other. If nothing else, Pearl would hear him chatting with the lady sheriff. She would then ask her grandson about Morgan's death, who in turn would tell one of the other four gossip queens. If not Aunt Fern, then someone else. Hopefully, the gossip would trickle down to my aunt and then to me. I did love a small town.

When I left, I looked over at the Howl at the Moon Wine and Cheese Emporium that Drake Harrison, my best male friend, owned. He'd just gotten the red and white striped awning cleaned, and I had to remember to tell him it looked great.

He was always my sounding board, and right now, I really needed one. Not that Aunt Fern didn't believe me about my ghost sighting, but she already believed in ghosts.

I crossed the street and entered the shop. Instead of Drake, his brother was there. "Jaxson? You're back!"

After the whole debacle with him being accused of killing the deputy, Drake's brother had left town, and I honestly didn't expect him to return. Ever. I was a bit hurt that Drake never told me that his brother was back. Drake and I shared everything—or so I had believed.

"Yeah. I went home for a couple of weeks, but then Drake said he could really use the help at the store. Apparently, his part time worker, Trace, decided to go back to school and had to cut down on his hours."

I had heard that—about Trace going back to school, not about Jaxson returning. "I'm very happy for you. Is Drake here?"

Jaxson looked off to the side. "No."

"When will he be back?"

"Soon." Jaxson was being rather cryptic. "Can I help you?"

Drake's brother wasn't the most unbiased person, but perhaps I could give him the low down without mentioning the part about seeing a ghost. "I'm trying to locate the wife of a man who recently died." Since Morgan's uncle was dead, my best bet was to find his aunt.

"Was he a friend of yours?"

"No." I told him about Floyd being mauled to death by wolves. "The strange part was that his house was ransacked. Wolves wouldn't do that."

He chuckled. "I take it you don't believe in werewolves?"

"Seriously? Not unless I see a person transform into one, I don't." Though before today, I didn't believe in ghosts. "Do you?"

"No! If you weren't friends with this Floyd guy, why the urge to find the wife?"

He sounded like everyone else. I'd eventually tell Drake about my ghost sighting. Since he'd tell Jaxson, it might be best to explain it to him first hand. "Because I met his nephew and he asked for my help."

"Then why not ask him for the whereabouts of his aunt?"

I blew out a breath. Since no one was in the store, I told him the whole story about the mix up with the potion—including meeting Aimee, the talking cat—and how I ran into Morgan the ghost. Throughout it all, Jaxson said nothing. "Well? Say something."

"Drake always said you had a fertile imagination."

"I would have agreed with you yesterday, but I know what I saw. How else would I know that Morgan Oliver had been shot and killed? He didn't live in town, so it wasn't like the rumor mill was up and running here."

A small smile stole across his lips. Jaxson knew all about gossip. "Did you do any research on the guy to see if he really is dead?"

"I did. And he is. Steve Rocker even confirmed it. The murder case is in the jurisdiction of the next county over, but since Morgan technically owns the Paxton farm now, his death is of interest to our sheriff. Those two are kind of working the case together—or at least that was what I got out of the conversation I had with him. I want to learn more about Morgan, which is why I plan to go over to his house and ask around about him."

Jaxson clenched his fists. "Are you crazy? Killers don't like people snooping around the crime scene. It could be dangerous."

"I don't know if Morgan's house is a crime scene. Morgan could have been killed anywhere, though most likely it was near Liberty. If he had been shot near his uncle's house, Witch's Cove's finest would have investigated the murder. Don't worry. I'm just going to drive by Morgan's house, not snoop inside. Afterward, I might even stop by the Liberty sheriff's department to see if they'll tell me anything."

"I'm coming with you."

I appreciated his concern, but I didn't really know Jaxson all that well. When I was fifteen, he went away to jail for a crime he didn't commit and only recently returned to Witch's Cove—once his record was expunged. Since he was Drake's brother, I probably should accept his offer. "What about the shop?"

"I'll put the closed sign up. Look, if anything happened to you and I didn't go, Drake would kill me. Literally."

Aw. My heart swelled. Drake cared. "Great. Let's go. I know the dead man's address. Maybe you should leave a note for Drake, so he doesn't wonder where you are."

"You don't need to tell me what to do," he snapped.

Ok-kay. That came out a bit too sharp. "Sorry," I said.

He dragged a hand down his jaw as he exhaled deeply. "No, I'm sorry. In prison, we were told what to do and when to do it. I had a little flashback just then."

"Duly noted. No giving directions. Got it."

His smile was brief. "Unless I ask."

I gave him a thumbs up.

Jaxson called Drake and told him that his brother's crazy sidekick was at it again, and that he intended to make sure I remained safe. While I couldn't hear what Drake was saying, he seemed to be agreeing with his brother.

Jaxson disconnected. "Let's go. I'm driving—and no arguing."

Darn. That would prevent me from doing something stupid—which I guess was a good thing.

It didn't take long to find Morgan Oliver's home two towns over. It was in a small subdivision with each home having a chain-linked fenced-in yard. The owners clearly took pride in their property since the lawns were cut and flowers abounded. I honestly couldn't imagine Morgan wanting to live on a hundred-acre farm if he had a ton of neighbors in this town. But what did I know? Maybe he planned to sell the place, or perhaps he needed more space. The man could be into motorcycles and want a shed to work on them. Sadly, I had no idea who Morgan Oliver really was.

"I'm parking a few houses away from Morgan's. We don't need to draw too much attention to ourselves." That sounded like someone familiar with the criminal system, and I had no problem with that.

I studied the area. One man, whose house sat next to Morgan's, was working on his car in his driveway. On the other side of Morgan's home was a woman rocking on her porch. No one else was outside.

I nodded to the mechanic. "Let me ask the questions, okay?" I asked. "You can be my muscle."

"Your muscle?" Jaxson grinned and flexed.

Okay, I have to admit, the guy was built. I laughed at his reaction, maybe a bit too loudly, and the man working on his car looked up. Since he didn't throw something at us or shoot us a deadly look, we approached him. "Hey there," I said.

"Can I help you?" He put the wrench he'd been using on the fender. I was happy he'd put the potential weapon away.

"I'm doing a newspaper story about Morgan Oliver's death. The cops don't seem to be getting anywhere with the investigation, and I was hoping you might be able to help." I have no idea why I said that, but thankfully Jaxson didn't mention that I was just a waitress in Witch's Cove.

"I'm not sure how. He kept to himself a lot, but he seemed like a good guy. I do know he had an uncle over in Witch's Cove. He'd go over there a lot to help the guy out after the man's wife died."

She died? That wasn't what the obituary implied, though one of the know-it-all Daniel sisters claimed she was dead—or rather might have been killed.

"That's nice to hear. Did Morgan have any enemies?"

"No." The man scratched his jaw. "Wait. I mean, there was a guy. Joe something. After Morgan's uncle passed away, he came around once. I know, because I heard shouting next door. When I asked Morgan about it later that day, he said the guy wanted to buy his uncle's farm. When Morgan said he didn't want to sell, the man wasn't pleased."

I hadn't heard about someone wanting to buy the farm. Our gossip ladies needed to step up their game. "Did Morgan plan to move to Witch's Cove and live on the farm?"

The car man shrugged. "I couldn't say. We honestly

didn't see a lot of each other. Besides, he was murdered the next day."

"In his house?" Jaxson asked.

"I don't know where it was. I mind my own business."

That was something he probably wanted us to do. "I appreciate your help, and I'm sorry for your loss." In all honesty, I don't know if he cared one way or the other. Having parents in the funeral business, the phrase had been ingrained in my brain since birth.

The man nodded and went back to work on his car. Jaxson and I left and headed toward the woman who lived on the other side of Morgan. As we walked by his white one-story home, a few trees obscured my view, but it looked as if his front door was ajar. I reached out and touched Jaxson's arm. "Does that door look open to you?"

"I don't think a ghost can open a door," Jaxson said with a slight quirk to his smile.

"He can't. At least I know Uncle Harold can't."

He immediately sobered. "Good to know, but that means…"

"Someone else is either in there, was in there, or the wind blew the door open," I said.

I took one step toward the house when Jaxson grabbed my arm. "That would be a no. You said you wouldn't snoop. It could be a maid for all we know. Let's ask the old lady on the porch. She seems to have an eagle eye."

I had to admit it was nice having someone with me who operated with a clearer head than me, but I don't know how he figured the porch neighbor knew something. Using all of my constraint, I didn't head up Morgan's driveway. "We should at least look in the mailbox," I said.

"If there is mail, do you plan on giving it to Morgan? It's probably ads that he can't take advantage of now or bills. You don't really believe he can do online banking or write a check, do you?"

I really hadn't thought through this ghost stuff. "No. I'm hoping he has a next of kin who can take care of this."

"Do you know who his lawyer is? Or who Floyd Paxton's lawyer was for that matter?"

"No, but I bet Steve knows."

"It's *Steve* now?" Jaxson asked.

"It's easier to refer to him by his first name, instead of by Sheriff Rocker. That's too many syllables."

Jaxson's face split into a full-blown smile. "You like him."

"I wish everyone would stop saying that. We've never gone out, and until today, I hadn't spoken to him since Cliff's murderer was brought to justice."

"Okay, I won't tease you anymore."

"Thank you." We reached the house where the elderly woman was sitting in her rocking chair.

When she saw us walk up the drive, she scowled. "If you're selling something, I don't want it," she shouted.

Okay, I hadn't expected that reaction. "We're not selling anything. We're here about Morgan Oliver," I called back.

Her face softened. I guess that was her way of welcoming us, so we continued up the porch steps but stopped before we came too close.

"What do you want to know?" Her tone was cautious at best.

"Do you know why Morgan's front door is open?" Jaxson

asked.

"No. I mind my own business—or least I have ever since Morgan was murdered. It was such a shame."

"Did you know him well?" I asked.

"I'd like to think so. He'd bring dinner over every once in a while. We'd eat and maybe even watch a movie together. I sure am going to miss him."

That was sad. "Did he have any enemies?"

"Morgan? No. He was the nicest guy in the world. Why he would help his uncle at his farm in Witch's Cove whenever he had the chance."

"I heard that," I said. "What about his aunt? I heard she died." I ignored the fact that the possibly erroneous obituary thought she was still alive.

The old lady leaned forward. "I guess now that Morgan's uncle is gone, I don't need to keep it a secret any longer."

I stepped closer. This could be the key I was looking for. "What secret?"

Chapter Six

"YOU CAN TELL us anything," I said. "We want whoever killed Morgan to pay for what he did."

The porch lady nodded. "His aunt is still alive."

That meant the Daniel sisters didn't know everything. "Do you know where she is living?"

"Phoenix."

Since this woman seemed to have inside knowledge, I wanted to learn as much as I could. "Do you know why she left Witch's Cove?"

"I've never met her, but Morgan said it was because his uncle was keeping secrets from her, and she didn't like it."

If that had been me, I might have tried to understand why he withheld information—not run away. But what was done was done. "I'm surprised Morgan helped his aunt's husband after that, if he was such a bad guy."

She nodded. "Me too, but Morgan could never say no to anyone in need."

He sounded like a saint, and people like that often led a double life. She coughed a few times and then wheezed. It was time to leave her in peace. "I appreciate your input. Have a nice day."

Jaxson's brows pinched. He must have thought I'd ask

more questions, but I'd had enough. I spun around and headed back to the car.

"What was the hurry?" Jaxson asked as he trotted after me.

"I don't know. I think she's the one who's hiding something."

"Whoa. Can you read minds now?" Jaxson asked as he caught up alongside of me.

"No, but something isn't right."

"About what?" Jaxson asked.

"Think of it this way. I'm Drake's friend, as well as yours, but I've known Drake longer."

"True, but where are you going with this?" he asked.

"Suppose you decided to steal something from Drake, or you beat him up. Because Drake is my friend, I'd stay away from you, even though you didn't personally harm me."

"Which means you find it odd that Morgan was nice to his uncle even after he harmed Morgan's aunt—at least emotionally?"

"Yes. If Morgan sided with the uncle, it was because Floyd Paxton didn't harm or lie to his wife. Instead, she did something to him. People keep secrets, you know."

"Drake is right. You have a creative mind."

"Maybe. I need more information. How about we stop at the sheriff's office to see what we can learn. Our pretense of going is to mention that Morgan's front door is open," I said.

"Let's do it." We reached Jaxson's car, and I slid into the passenger seat. Not knowing where the sheriff's department was located, I opened the Waze app on my phone, found its location, and gave Jaxson directions.

It wasn't far to the main part of town. My first impression of Liberty was a good one. The one and two-story storefronts were quaint, or should I say downright homey? It looked like the people liked their town to look nice too.

Jaxson parked in front of the sheriff's department. When we entered the brick building, we asked to speak with the sheriff since she was already working the case with Steve.

"What is this about?" the receptionist asked.

"Morgan Oliver's murder."

Her eyes widened. I might have stretched the truth a bit, but she might not know that Morgan's aunt was still alive and living in Phoenix. It was also possible no one here was aware of the fight Morgan had a day before he was shot. With only having Joe's first name, it wouldn't help that much though.

She called the sheriff and then disconnected. "Sheriff Willows will be right out. Can I have your names?"

Both of us supplied the requested information, as well as provided phone numbers.

Before we could sit down, a very pretty brunette with her hair done up in a French twist walked down the hallway wearing a beige body-hugging uniform. "I'm Sheriff Willows. You have information on Morgan Oliver's murder?" Her tone was professional, yet a bit distant.

"I think so," I said, hoping I had something useful.

"Come into my office."

I looked up at Jaxson, wondering if being in a law enforcement office was bothering him considering he might be remembering how Sheriff Duncan had treated him eleven years ago. From his calm outer appearance, it didn't. Good for him.

The sheriff closed her door and motioned we take a seat. "What do you know about Morgan Oliver's death?" she asked, getting straight to the point. I liked that.

I was just about to dive in when Jaxson spoke up. "We were driving by his house and noticed his front door was open. Seeing how he's passed, we thought we should mention it."

The sheriff's face paled. "Did you see anyone around? Or did you look inside?"

We both shook our heads. "No." This time I answered.

"Excuse me for one second while I ask someone to investigate." The sheriff called an officer and told him to check it out. She disconnected and then faced us. "Did you know Mr. Oliver?"

I jumped in. "Not exactly." I introduced both of us, telling her we lived in Witch's Cove. "When I heard that Floyd Paxton was mauled to death, it was rather unsettling. Wolves—especially ones that attack—would be terrible for tourism."

"I agree. But what's the interest in Mr. Oliver? He's from Liberty."

I really wanted to tell her what the ghost had said, but I couldn't bring myself to do it. I didn't know Misty Willows, so I couldn't judge if she'd be receptive or not. "When I found out someone had broken into Floyd's house and then his favorite relative was murdered shortly thereafter, I wanted to help."

"I see. Is there anything you know that I might not be aware of about this case?"

I looked over to Jaxson. He must have thought that meant

it was his cue to talk. "Only that according to his one neighbor, there had been a man named Joe who visited Mr. Oliver's house the day before he was murdered," Jaxson said. "Apparently, Joe wanted to buy Floyd Paxton's farm, but Morgan wasn't willing to sell. The discussion became rather heated."

"I am aware of that altercation."

"Was Morgan's house trashed?" I asked.

"I'm afraid so. Do you have any idea what this person might have been looking for?"

"I wish I did. It's possible it was the same person or people who trashed his uncle's place."

"I see. Well, thank you," Sheriff Willows said. "And thanks for telling us about the robbery," the sheriff said.

"Sure thing." I had hoped the sheriff would have said she'd keep us in the loop, but she didn't. Since she was working with Steve, I bet she'd tell him what was going on. And that meant, I might find out about the conversation.

As if Jaxson could read my mind about needing to leave, he pushed back his chair and stood. When he shook the sheriff's hand, I swear she inwardly swooned. They were both about the same age, and Jaxson was quite handsome. Having him around had turned out to have been a smart move on my part.

Just as we stepped outside of the sheriff's department, a man who was dressed in black slacks and a light weight white shirt approached the building and then climbed the steps. My blood pressure dropped, and my heart beat hard. It was Morgan Oliver—only this time he was very much alive.

I grabbed Jaxson's arm to stop him. He turned to me.

"Did you forget something?" he asked.

"No." I could barely say that word. The man was Morgan Oliver's double. When he didn't even look our way, I had to find out if I had lost my mind, so I called his name. "Morgan?"

The man stopped and faced me. "Did you just call me Morgan?"

"I did." I really wanted to reach out and touch him to make sure he was solid, but I didn't dare.

He bit down on his lip. "I believe Morgan is my twin brother—or rather was. Did you know him?"

My knees weakened. Had it not been for Jaxson wrapping a supportive arm around my waist, I might have dropped to the ground. "Kind of."

"Do you two have a moment to chat?" the doppelganger asked. "I came here looking for answers about his death."

My mouth was so dry, I had a hard time moving my lips. Thankfully, Jaxson jumped in to the rescue. "We did too. We live in Witch's Cove. How about grabbing a coffee?"

"That would be great. The heat is a bit intense in the sun."

That implied he wasn't from here. Or was he? Right now, my mind wasn't thinking clearly. I did a quick mental scan of the streets. "I think we passed a coffee shop on our way over here."

"Sounds perfect," Morgan's twin said.

I led the way, and Jaxson told him our names.

"Nice to meet you. I'm Trevor Whitehall."

Why didn't they have the same last name? They sure looked like twins. Duh. "Were you adopted?"

"I was, but my adoptive parents told me I was an only child. It wasn't until last week that I just happened to see something on the news about Morgan Oliver's death. I thought I was imagining things when I saw what looked like my face staring back at me."

"That must have freaked you out."

He chuckled. "You could say that."

They reached a rather cute looking coffee shop with a red door and a new-looking black and white awning. While the three outside café tables were in the shade, I figured we'd be more comfortable sitting inside in the air-conditioned space. I knew I'd enjoy it more.

Once we grabbed an inside table, I ordered a sweet tea, Jaxson asked for a Coke, and Trevor wanted a hot coffee.

"I was on my way into the sheriff's department to find out more about my twin, when you called Morgan's name. I'd say that constituted a psychic event. What can you tell me about him?" he asked.

Since Jaxson had been visiting his parents in Orlando during the time Floyd Paxton was killed, I probably could fill in the blanks better. "A few weeks ago, a man by the name of Floyd Paxton was attacked and killed by wolves."

"Who is that?"

"Morgan's uncle. I honestly have no idea if Morgan knew anything about the circumstances of his birth."

"That must have been tough on him to lose a loved one. Go on."

I could discuss the break-ins in both homes, but Trevor wouldn't have any idea what might have been taken. The only way we could help each other was if I came clean. "I need to tell you the whole truth about me and Morgan. You will think I'm just some kook, but trust me, I'm not."

"Tell me."

I glanced over at Jaxson. With raised brows, he held up his hands. "Go for it. You have nothing to lose."

I agreed. I started at the beginning—or sort of at the beginning. "There was this magic potion I needed for a spell. I'm a witch by the way." When he didn't even blink at the piece of news, I continued. "That spell involved me ingesting this potion. All would have been fine and dandy, had the witch who made it not inadvertently mixed the wrong ingredients. Long story short, the side effect of that mistake enabled me to see dead people—your twin brother's ghost to be exact."

Trevor remained quiet for a moment. The server delivered our drinks and then asked if we wanted something to eat. I didn't. My stomach was already in knots. Once I declined, the two men did too.

Trevor inhaled. "When you saw him, were you able to communicate with him?" I could tell by the slow way he delivered his words that he was finding my story difficult to believe, but I had to give him credit. He didn't laugh at me.

"We did, but it took a lot of energy on his part. He said someone had shot him in the back. When he twisted around, I could see the blood stain. I think he was so excited that he was visible to someone that he asked me to help him find out who had murdered him."

Trevor blew on his hot coffee and then took a sip. "To be clear, a complete stranger walked up to you, told you someone murdered him, and asked for your help?"

"I wouldn't say he actually walked up to me. More like he appeared out of nowhere. And he was fairly translucent." If he wasn't before, I think Trevor was reevaluating my sanity.

He cleared his throat. "Why would you help him if you'd never met him before?"

"I got this," Jaxson said. "Glinda is incapable of keeping her nose out of other people's business. Though if she hadn't decided it was her job—as a waitress—to help solve a recent murder case, I, instead of the real killer, might be in jail right now."

"You're an amateur sleuth?" Trevor asked.

Iggy thought he was, but I hadn't even considered it—until now. "Maybe."

"Good enough for me. What did my twin's ghost say exactly?"

"Just that he'd inherited his uncle's farm. I'm not even sure if it had gone through the courts before your brother was killed."

"Do the police have a suspect?"

"Not that I know of," I said. "Maybe that's why Morgan needed my help. I imagine he tried to contact someone here in Liberty, but apparently he wasn't able to find anyone who could see him."

"I see," Trevor said.

"Because Morgan's uncle lived in my town, he might have thought someone there could help. We are known for our extensive talents in the witch department," I said.

"That makes sense. Did he say anything else?"

"No. The sheriff from my town showed up in the middle of our conversation, and Morgan disappeared." I drank most of my iced tea and Jaxson downed his soda. Because the air was thick with uncertainty and disbelief, I wanted to put Trevor on the hotseat for a change. "Can I ask what you do for a living?"

"I'm a sales representative for a medical imaging company. What did Morgan do?"

How sad was it that I didn't know? "I'm not sure." I pulled out the paper with Morgan's home address on it and handed it to Trevor. "This was where he lived. The elderly woman next door seems to have been close to him. She would know."

Trevor pocketed the piece of paper. "I really appreciate your input and your willingness to help. I'd like to stay in touch. Let's exchange phone numbers."

I found out that Trevor lived in Pine Grove, which was only about fifty miles from Liberty. What a shame that the two brothers lived so close, yet were unaware of each other. After we settled our bill, Jaxson and I left.

Once in the car, he glanced over at me. "Was this trip worth it?" he asked.

"Totally. Meeting the ghost's twin was a bit unsettling though."

"I can only imagine," Jaxson said as he started the engine. "What's your next step in solving the crime?"

He acted like I believed I was the lead on the case. "Nothing."

Jaxson chuckled. "Glinda Goodall, you aren't capable of letting this go."

"I want to let it go and let the two departments handle everything, but now that I've met Morgan's twin, I feel more connected to the case than ever. I can't ignore it."

Jaxson grinned. "That's my girl."

What did that mean? The two of us didn't even know each other that well. "From the safety of my home, I want to see if I can find Emma Paxton. Like I said, something seems off about Morgan's relationship with his uncle."

"Maybe he didn't like his aunt. Who's to say she didn't run away with another man."

"You could absolutely be right," I said.

Jaxson didn't say anything for a few minutes. Thinking he might need some time to put things in perspective, I kept quiet too.

"Did you know that after I decided not to become a lawyer, I studied computer science?" he blurted.

What? "Drake never told me."

"That's because I never told him."

"Why would you keep that from him? Going back to school is a huge accomplishment."

Jaxson looked over at me. "Remember, I was the ex-con. I didn't want to mess up what my brother had built in Witch's Cove. It was why I didn't communicate with him very often."

"I, for one, think it's cool that you didn't let your past get in your way of an education."

"Thanks." He ran his hand along the steering wheel. "Listen, I want to help with the Oliver case."

Stun me now. "Really? Why?"

He shrugged. "I don't have any direction in my life right now. Don't get me wrong, I like working for my brother, but my goal would not be to stock wine or order different cheeses for the rest of my life."

"I don't know. Free wine for life sounds good to me." I wanted to lighten the mood a bit.

He laughed, as I had hoped. "Just so you know, Drake charges me for the wine."

"Oh." I didn't want to get into those family dynamics. "How do you think you could help? It's not like you can see Morgan."

"No, but I am a whiz on the computer. After I finished school, I worked at a tech company. I was relegated to doing rather low-level projects because of my record, but I learned a lot. I can try to locate Emma Paxton for you."

"That would be great. I'm good with technology—sort of—but hacking into any kind of database is not in my genes."

He chuckled. "I get it. Let's keep this between the two of us. I don't want Drake to think I'm slacking."

Now it was Jaxson who was being funny. "Deal."

Chapter Seven

JAXSON PARKED IN front of the wine and cheese store. Because the sign on the front was down, Drake must have returned. Just as I slipped out, I had an idea. "Do you have five minutes to check something out?" I asked.

"Sure. What's up?"

"I want to go across the street to the parking lot. Maybe Morgan will show up. If he does, I want to ask him a few more questions."

"Works for me. If Morgan knows his aunt's new address, it will save me some time."

"Wouldn't that be nice."

I felt a little silly attempting to contact a ghost. Truth was, I wasn't even sure how to go about it. For all I knew, the ghost could teleport all over the world in seconds and not even be anywhere near Witch's Cove right now. My best bet was to return to the spot where I saw him last.

"Now what?" Jaxson asked.

"Face me in case Morgan appears. I don't want people to think I'm talking to myself."

He flashed me a smile. "You are a trip."

"I'm serious. Just so you know, I've never summoned a ghost before." I couldn't help myself from glancing at the sheriff's department, hoping Steve didn't come out. I didn't need him to have any more ammunition about how crazy I was.

"Morgan?" I whispered. "I need to talk to you. It's about your case."

If he was around, I figured that would draw him out. Something cold touched my face, and I immediately wiped it away. "Sorry. Is that you?"

"Is he here?" Jaxson asked. He sounded sincere.

"I don't see him, but I think I felt him."

Something next to Jaxson wavered and then formed. "What did you find out?" the ghost asked. "If I go in and out, keep talking."

I looked over at Jaxson. "He's here. Okay, I learned a lot today, just not who killed you." I had a few suspects, but I didn't want to get his hopes up. "We spoke to two of your neighbors. The man next to you said you and some guy by the name of Joe fought with you. What was his last name? And do you think he might have wanted to kill you?"

I realize that was a lot to ask all at once, but I feared he might disappear before I was ready. When Morgan didn't answer, my hope drained.

"Delaney," the voice said. "Joe Delaney. He has the property adjacent my uncle's farm. And yes, he's my first choice as to who would want me dead."

"Thank you." I repeated it so that Jaxson would help me remember the name in case I forgot.

To my surprise, Jaxson pulled out his phone and pressed record. I felt a little better knowing I had a backup. "Do you know who the farm would go to, now that you're…ah…not around anymore?"

"I didn't have a will, so no. I'm guessing my aunt. Her name might be on the lease. Or maybe Uncle Floyd's brother. You should ask Sandy Vickers, my uncle's lawyer."

That was such good intel that I repeated the tidbit to Jaxson in case he wanted to ask a question. "The lady on the other side told us your aunt was living in Phoenix. You don't think she could have had anything to do with your death, do you?" I asked Morgan.

"Absolutely not."

When he didn't elaborate, I continued. "Why did she really leave Witch's Cove?"

"I wish I knew. Uncle Floyd wouldn't say, but I had the sense it was her choice."

Maybe she'd done something she wasn't proud of. Morgan's image started to go in and out again. I had to hurry. "You'll never guess who I met today."

I waited for Morgan to ask who, but his image vanished and the brush of cold on my cheek implied he was gone.

"He left," I told Jaxson. "It seems like he only has enough energy to stay for a short time. Darn it." Jaxson didn't say anything for a minute, and I didn't blame him. That was a lot to process.

"You should have asked if he knew his aunt's address."

I snapped my fingers and groaned. "I forgot. Darn it. Next time, I'll write down my questions before I contact him."

He stared at me for a few seconds. "You really can talk to ghosts, can't you?"

"At least to two of them."

"I'll check out Joe Delaney to see what his story is," Jaxson said.

A couple walked out of the Bubbling Cauldron Coffee Shop, which meant it was time to skedaddle. "Do you think Drake will believe us?" I asked.

"Us?"

He had a point. "Me."

"Drake trusts you. I bet he will, but he'll caution you to be careful. Sticking your nose where it doesn't belong could get you in trouble."

"I know. I will take my findings to our sheriff when I'm a bit more sure about my facts."

Jaxson nodded. "Smart."

"I'm going to head back," I said.

"I thought you wanted to talk to Drake," he said.

"I do, but you can tell him everything."

"Sure. I'll do some research and let you know," Jaxson said.

"I appreciate it."

Jaxson headed to the wine and cheese store while I returned to the Tiki Hut Grill building. As much as I wanted to get Aunt Fern's take on things—and maybe Uncle Harold's—I needed a moment to think things through. I stopped in my tracks. Uh-oh. If I went home, Iggy would grill me, and I wasn't ready for that either.

I did an about face. Because I was hungry, I headed to the Spellbound Diner. Sure, I could have grabbed some food for free at the Tiki Hut, but I wanted the solace—and, you guessed it, some gossip. Who better to talk to than the owner, Dolly Andrews, one of the five gossip queens of Witch's Cove?

I already knew that Miriam Daniels wasn't in the know about Emma Paxton. She thought Morgan's aunt was dead. There was no way I could come out and ask Pearl—not with her grandson sitting close by. The sheriff already seemed upset with her inability to keep quiet.

The diner it was.

As much as I didn't want to admit it, the interior was really cute. Don't get me wrong. The Tiki Hut Grill was cute too, what with its movie and beach theme, but this small place had a kitschy charm all of its own. It had red leather Naugahyde-covered booths situated along the window, black and white checkered walls, and chrome everywhere else. Only three of the ten booths were occupied. I sat in one as far from the others as possible.

As soon as Dolly spotted me, she rushed over. "My, oh, my. If it isn't Glinda Goodall. If Fern was dead, she'd be rolling over in her grave. What are you doing here?" The delight in her voice was rather cute.

"I just need a place to think."

Her eyes sparkled. "Think about what?"

Dolly was a witch, and as such, wouldn't laugh at my ability to talk to ghosts. I feared though that she'd tell all of Witch's Cove about the sighting. However, if I had any hope of finding out about this murder, I had to put my embarrassment aside.

"It's about Floyd Paxton."

"That old coot?"

No one seemed to like him, but he must have had some redeeming qualities if his nephew frequently helped him out. "Yeah. I heard his nephew was murdered about a week later—

shot in the back no less."

"This is good stuff. Let me get you something, and we can chat. It's on the house."

Oh, boy. I probably should say no, but I wanted her information as much as she wanted mine. "A sweet tea and a grilled cheese sandwich with tomato."

Dolly grinned. "Coming right up."

I wasn't sure I was doing the right thing talking to Dolly. I almost felt as if I was going behind Aunt Fern's back. The two used to have a big rivalry—mostly over Uncle Harold—but now it was about who ran the best restaurant. As if Dolly's ten-booth diner could compete with Aunt Fern's large restaurant. Not a chance.

Half expecting a call from Drake once his brother explained what was going on, I placed my phone on the table.

One of Dolly's servers brought over my drink. "Your grilled cheese is coming right up," she said with a smile.

"Thanks."

While I waited for my meal, I went over everything that had happened today—from meeting a ghost, telling Aunt Fern about it, and then joining forces with Jaxson, of all people, to find more information. I had to admit Jaxson had been a big help. Not only was he strong enough to keep me out of harm's way, he didn't try to take over the investigation. I never expected someone with a chip on his shoulder to let a female take the lead. Though after he was finally found innocent of the liquor store robbery from eleven years ago, his attitude had changed—for the better, I might add.

Dolly placed my grilled cheese on the table and then slipped into the booth across from me. "Spill."

I had to laugh at her direct approach. "What do you know about Floyd's wife, who by the way, is living in Phoenix."

She snapped her fingers. "I knew it."

I took a bite out of my sandwich and moaned. "This is really good."

"Thanks. You should eat here more often."

I smiled. "I'll think about it." Or not. Aunt Fern wouldn't be happy. "Tell me why you knew Emma Paxton wasn't dead like Miriam Daniels believed."

Dolly leaned forward. "I think she was having an affair. I mean, who couldn't blame her? Floyd had issues."

"Issues? What kind of issues?"

"He would go off somewhere every month and wouldn't tell Emma what he was up to."

I had to think about that for a moment. "Wouldn't that imply that he was the one who was having the affair?"

"Hmm. Maybe you're right. I'm not sure."

So much for that line of inquiry. "Do you know a Joe Delaney?"

"Sure do."

I waited for Dolly to continue, but she must want me to drag it out of her. That would give her the upper hand. "I heard he was pretty adamant about buying Floyd's ranch—all one hundred acres of it."

"I had heard that too."

Really? Then why hadn't Aunt Fern known? She was slipping.

"Where does Joe live?" I knew, but I wanted to test her.

Her eyes widened, acting as if everyone knew. "Next door to Floyd, of course. I heard Joe was looking to expand his operation."

Dolly did seem to know a few things. "What can you tell me about Floyd's nephew—the one who stood to inherit the farm?"

"Nothing. I never met him. Who will get the farm now that he's dead?" she asked.

That was the big question. "I don't know. I read that Floyd has a brother. Do you know anything about him?"

"Just that he lives over in Winston. I don't think Floyd and Charles got along though."

Winston was about an hour south of here. "Good to know."

Dolly sat back. "Why the sudden interest in Floyd?"

"It's a long story." I quickly stuffed my face with my sandwich in order to keep from spilling my guts.

"I love long stories."

Dolly was known for her way-out thinking. She claimed she'd had some out-of-body experiences and had even met an alien once. I finished the first half of my sandwich and washed it down with my drink. As much as I didn't want to tell her, having another set of eyes and ears would make it easier. "Have you ever seen a ghost?"

"A ghost? Like the way your aunt can see your Uncle Harold?"

"Yes."

"I have," she announced with pride.

My pulse soared. "Was your ghost kind of transparent?"

"He was, unless his sister was nearby."

What did one have to do with the other? "I don't understand."

"If a blood relative is near a ghost, the deceased can draw power from that relative. Why are you asking? Have you seen a ghost?"

Dolly seemed safe enough. "Yes, but please don't tell anyone. It could be harmful to my health."

"Oh, my." Dolly made a zipping motion over her lips. "Who did you see?"

I leaned forward. "Morgan Oliver. Emma Paxton's nephew," I whispered.

"The one who just died?" Her voice trailed off.

"Yes. I met him this morning. Across the street in the parking lot."

"What did he say?" she asked bubbling with excitement.

I was pleased she didn't ask how I was suddenly able to see him. Not only was I rather tired of telling that story, Hazel's reputation would be ruined if word got out. "Not much, other than someone shot him in the back, and he asked me to help find the killer."

"You?"

She didn't have to sound so indignant. "I helped find out who killed Cliff."

"I did hear you were instrumental in bringing the killer to justice."

"I was, and now I want to help Morgan. I thought maybe you could ask around about him."

Dolly smiled. "Why, I'd love to. Nothing like a good murder to get my juices flowing. What does the handsome sheriff have to say about this?"

"He and the sheriff over in Liberty, where Morgan lived, have joined forces."

"Oh, really? I've heard she's a real looker." She wiggled her brows.

If Dolly was trying to make me jealous, she failed. "She is pretty."

"Okay, so what's our first move?"

Chapter Eight

WE? I WAVED a hand at Dolly. "There's nothing we can do for now. In fact, it's been one dead end after another." There were a lot of dead ends, but Jaxson and I had made progress. I wasn't sure I wanted Dolly involved more than asking a few questions. "Floyd was killed by wolves, so his death has been solved. Sure, the sheriff is still investigating who broke into Floyd's house, but does it really matter now? If the thief was looking for something, he either found it or it wasn't there in the first place." I didn't really mean that. All criminals needed to be brought to justice, but I wanted Dolly to focus on Morgan's murder.

"What about his nephew? You told Morgan that you'd help. Are you going to give up?" Dolly asked.

Darn. She caught me. If I said I would stop investigating, then Dolly might be the one to find the killer, and I couldn't have that—for my aunt's sake, of course. "Jaxson is trying to locate his aunt. She might have some answers."

"What about talking to Joe?"

I didn't know him at all, but then an idea struck. I had to return to work tomorrow and really didn't have the time to run down every lead. "Do you know him very well?"

"Sort of. He comes in here every once in a while."

"If you really want to help, how about talking to him? The sheriff over in Liberty knows about him. I'm guessing Sheriff Rocker has asked him a few questions too, but you and I both know that people are often skittish around the law."

"You are so right, Glinda. Let me see what I can do. This is so exciting. But do me a favor."

"Sure. What is it?"

"Don't tell your aunt. She'll be so jealous that I'm going to help solve a crime. I don't need her snooping around too."

I laughed. "You two are way too competitive."

"We are that, so can you keep a lid on it?" Dolly asked.

"I'll do my best." At least I hoped I could keep my mouth shut. If Dolly was instrumental in helping me solve the crime, I bet my aunt would be the first person Dolly bragged to.

Dolly left to take care of her diner while I finished my meal. Even though she said the meal was on the house, I left enough cash to cover my bill, along with a nice tip.

Since the wine and cheese store sat between Dolly's diner and the Tiki Hut Grill, I decided to stop in and fill the men in on what Dolly said. When I entered, I was happy to see no customers were there—happy that I could chat with them, not happy no one was at Drake's store. He claimed that most of the sales happen between dinner time and ten at night. He also said that Friday and Saturday were his big days. Today was only Wednesday.

Drake smiled. "I hear you and my brother had quite the adventure today."

"That would be an understatement. A failed potion for Iggy, a ghost sighting, and then the search for a killer."

I waited for Drake to tell me I was crazy, but he didn't.

"Where did you go after we spoke with Morgan?" Jaxson asked as he entered from the back hallway.

We spoke to the ghost? He couldn't hear or see him, but I appreciated that Jaxson took me seriously. "I decided to grab a bite to eat at the Spellbound Diner."

Drake's eyes sparkled. "Smart. What did Dolly have to say about all this?"

I gave them both the rundown.

"I'll try to find an address for Charles Paxton too," Jaxson said.

While I already knew where Joe Delaney lived, I couldn't be more pleased that he was willing to spend the time to help. "I love that Dolly will pick Joe Delaney's brain. She can be pretty persuasive when she wants to be."

The brothers nodded. "No kidding. What are we doing next?" Drake asked.

"You're helping too?"

"While I have a business to run, I'm always a good sounding board. Besides, I think it's cool you can talk to a ghost."

"Thanks." I remembered what Dolly said. "What we need is for Trevor to help us."

"What can he do?" Jaxson asked.

"According to Dolly, if the ghost is near a blood relative, Morgan can draw energy from him. That might give Morgan the ability to last a bit longer in his visible form."

"If that happens, maybe he won't disappear before we've finished asking our questions," Jaxson said. "If Morgan can feed off of Trevor's energy, do you think it's possible that I could see him?"

I doubted that, though I loved how onboard Jaxson was.

"We'll see. Right now, I need a nap. My brain is fried."

Jaxson nodded. "I'll let you know what I find out about Emma Paxton's location, and if I find anything useful about Joe Delaney or Floyd's brother, Charles."

"You might as well add in Trevor Whitehall. I'm not positive he is exactly who he says he is."

Jaxson's cheer disappeared. "You don't think he killed his own brother—a brother he only learned existed a few days ago, do you?"

"I'm going to keep an open mind. In the meantime, I'll check with Sandy Vickers tomorrow to see who stands to inherit the farm now that Floyd and Morgan are dead."

"She's a lawyer, right?" Jaxson asked.

"Yes." I was surprised he didn't know of her until I remembered that Jaxson had moved away from Witch's Cove many years ago.

"Why not ask *Steve*?" Jaxson said. For a moment, he almost sounded jealous, which was totally ridiculous. Drake's brother always considered me like a little sister.

"I just might." I gave him a quick smile. "Thanks again for your help."

"Anytime."

I left by the beachside door and walked past my parent's funeral home to the Tiki Hut Grill. When I entered through the side entrance, I peeked into the restaurant. Anna Butler, one of the evening servers, was handling the cash register, which meant Aunt Fern was upstairs. When my aunt needed a break, the servers took their turn checking people out. While the work was easier than waitressing, there were fewer tips.

I trudged upstairs, knowing I'd be grilled by Iggy as soon

as I walked through the door. Not wanting to tell the story twice, I knocked on Aunt Fern's door first.

"Glinda! You're back. I was worried about you."

Good to know. I'd already gone over my meeting with Morgan earlier. What she didn't know was what Jaxson and I learned. "How about I invite Iggy over? I can tell both of you what I learned at the same time."

"Perfect."

As I stepped away from Aunt Fern's door to go to my apartment, my very cute but curious iguana came out of the cat door. He looked up at me with fake innocence as if he wasn't about to head out and cause trouble. Iggy never liked it when I was gone all day. "Where are you going, young man?" I asked. "Off to see Aimee?"

"I already saw her, and I apologized."

That surprised me. "And?"

I waited for him to tell me Aimee had accepted his remorse, but he apparently decided to be closed mouthed—a rare condition for him. "Nothing."

I knew that no amount of prying would do me any good. "I'm about to tell Aunt Fern about my day. Would you like to join us?"

His sour attitude disappeared. "Yes!"

Iggy rushed across the hall and jumped through her cat door before I'd taken a step. I went to Aunt Fern's apartment, lightly knocked, and opened the door.

"Some sweet tea?" she asked.

"That would be wonderful. I've had a stressful day."

Aunt Fern turned to Iggy. "And for you, my cute little man? Some hibiscus flowers?"

My aunt went to great lengths to make my familiar happy.

"Yes, please," he said. I swear he was only polite when Aunt Fern was around.

"You spoil him, you know," I said.

"He's worth it," my aunt called from the kitchen.

Naturally, Iggy loved that. He stuck his tongue out at me, and I did the same back to him. Aunt Fern carried out the drinks along with Iggy's flower on a saucer. She held up a finger. "I want Harold to hear this."

"Won't that tire him?" I asked.

"Yes, but he doesn't have to be in his full human form if he doesn't want to be." She turned toward the bedroom. "Harold? Your niece is here to tell us about her ghost sighting."

My aunt hadn't turned around before Uncle Harold materialized. His open arms and warm smile had me jumping to my feet. I'd taken a step when I realized that if I'd tried to hug him, I'd only be grasping at air. Darn.

"Uncle Harold?" Iggy said.

"Yes, it's Uncle Harold," I answered. "You can see him?"

"I can. I can. At least sort of," Iggy said.

It had never occurred to me that he might be able to see a ghost too, but it made sense. He drank the same potion I did. "Uncle Harold, say something to Iggy."

"How have you been, my boy? You look very handsome."

My uncle was the best. I knew how much those words meant to my familiar. If Iggy could hear him, he'd answer.

My familiar looked over at me, and I swear he almost turned green. "I'm great, thank you."

My muscles almost melted. "I can't believe we all can see you, Uncle Harold."

"It sure is a relief. It makes it almost okay to be dead."

I chuckled, thinking he meant that as a joke.

"Tell us what you found out about our dead man." Aunt Fern must have decided that gossip was more important than our family reunion.

I explained about revealing to Sheriff Rocker that I'd seen a ghost. "He kept focusing on what Morgan Oliver was wearing though."

"Why of course, dear," my aunt said.

"Why is that?"

"If you could describe what Morgan Oliver was wearing at the time of his death then he'd have to believe you."

Wow. I hadn't considered that. "Uncle Harold. Can you change clothes if you want to?"

"No, my dear."

"Does that mean Morgan Oliver will have to wear a bloodied white T-shirt for the rest of his time on Earth?" I wasn't sure if when he crossed over whether his body disappeared or not.

"I'm afraid so."

Hmm. Maybe Aunt Fern was right. If I had the clothing details correct, Steve would have to at least consider that I might be telling the truth—or had somehow sneaked a peek at the crime scene photos.

"Did our esteemed sheriff know anything that was helpful?" Aunt Fern asked.

"Just that he is working with the sheriff over in Liberty. She is working on Morgan's death while Steve is still trying to find out who robbed Floyd Paxton."

What followed was a serious of questions about the female sheriff, but I really didn't want to get into whether or not I thought she and Steve had a thing for each other. It was none of my business.

"After my chat with our esteemed lawman, I went to talk to Drake."

"He's always been your go-to guy, hasn't he?" my aunt asked.

She understood how important our friendship was. "Yes. Only Drake wasn't there—Jaxson was."

She nodded. "I'd heard he was back."

"Why didn't you tell me he'd come home?"

"I thought Drake would have mentioned it. In fact, I was a bit upset that I had to hear it from Dolly, and you know how much it galls me to not be the first in the know."

The rivalry continued. "Why, yes I do. I can see we need to work harder at communicating."

"We sure do," she said.

Iggy grunted. "And I'll keep you in the loop too."

He lifted his upper body. "You better. Don't forget how talented I am about finding information."

"You are." His clues had helped solve Cliff's murder.

That led me to wonder how valuable a ghost could be. "Uncle Harold, if I wanted you to spy on someone, could you do that?" I had no idea what his abilities were.

"I could, but I wouldn't since I don't think it's right."

Good old Uncle Harold. I bet he'd do whatever Aunt Fern asked him to do though. "Good to know. Anyway, back to my day. I told everything to Jaxson—including talking to the ghost. When I said I wanted to question some of Morgan's neighbors, Jaxson kind of freaked, saying it might be dangerous."

"I'm glad he did," Uncle Harold said. "You have no idea how many crazies there are out there these days."

Considering Morgan had been shot in the back, my uncle might be right. "Which was why Jaxson insisted on coming with me."

"Good for him," my aunt said.

I explained how we drove to Morgan's neighborhood, met two of his neighbors, and what they told us.

"Emma Paxton is alive? Well, I'll be," Aunt Fern said.

"Apparently." I told her that Jaxson is going to see if he can find her address. I also mentioned that since Morgan's front door was open, we were obligated to go to town to report it.

"Very clever way of worming your way into the sheriff's department. Did she tell you anything?" my aunt asked.

"No." I didn't refute the fact that I had used the possible break-in as a way to find out something, because that was true. I then told them about meeting Morgan's twin on the steps of the sheriff's department. "I swear I thought Morgan had come back to life."

"He has a twin? I never knew that, but if Harold's twin ever showed up, it would scare me for sure," Aunt Fern said.

"I don't have a twin," Harold shot back.

Aunt Fern waved a hand. "It was just an example. Since Trevor didn't know about Morgan until now, I bet Morgan didn't know about Trevor either."

"You're probably right," I said. "We filled Trevor in the

best we could, though there wasn't all that much to tell. When Jaxson and I returned to town, we went to where I saw Morgan the first time, and I called out to him. I had more questions for Morgan after visiting Liberty."

"That's good that you returned to where you first saw him. We often hang out in the same spot," Uncle Harold said.

I liked that I had a resident expert in house. "I'll keep that in mind." I explained that he said Joe Delaney wanted to buy his uncle's land, but that Floyd had turned him down. When Joe asked Morgan about selling, he said no too. According to one neighbor, Joe got really mad."

"If anyone tried to take the Tiki Hut from me, I'd put up a fight," she said.

Taking and buying weren't the same thing, but I held my tongue. "Morgan said that Sandy Vickers was his uncle's attorney. I'm hoping she'll know something."

"That's good, dear. Great work. It seems as if Jaxson was quite a help today."

"He was. I never would have guessed it." I snapped my fingers, pretending as if what I was about to say was a side note. "I probably shouldn't mention this, but I went to see Dolly a few minutes ago."

I waited for the disapproval. My aunt looked over to where Uncle Harold had been floating. Even though he was no longer visible, I sensed he was still there.

"Uncle Harold, why do you keep disappearing? Can't you feed off of my energy since we're blood relatives?"

My heart fluttered and my breath caught. Then my uncle appeared. "I can, but I don't like to. I've heard it's not very pleasant for the relative."

Uncle Harold remained visible, but I could feel his presence. It wasn't enjoyable, but I didn't mind. "It's not bad."

My aunt lifted her chin. "Did Dolly have anything to add?"

"Just that she'll talk to Joe Delaney to see why he wanted that land so badly."

"She's a good person to do that. What are you planning next?"

"After talking to the attorney tomorrow? I have no idea."

Chapter Nine

THE NEXT DAY at work was so slow that it forced me to go over what happened yesterday many, many times. I still couldn't believe I could see and talk to ghosts. It was crazy. I probably should have asked Hazel if there was a time limit on my ability to see them. I hoped not. I liked having access to the dead.

The dead! How could I have forgotten that my mom could connect with them? She might not be able to see them, but perhaps she could contact Morgan if he didn't have enough energy to appear. I could ask him questions through her. While her discussion with our deceased deputy a few weeks ago had some inaccuracies, Morgan might be more forthcoming if he understood it was to help with his case.

Penny, my best girlfriend, placed a hand on my arm. "Hey, you okay?"

"I'm fine, why?"

"You've been quiet all day."

I pulled her over to the coffee stand. "That's because I promised Iggy I would try to do a spell to turn him green."

"Oh, no. That's terrible."

Penny loved that Iggy was pink. "I know, but he's been begging me forever. But don't worry, Hazel mixed up the ingredients, and the spell didn't work." That was the truth—just not all of it.

I probably should have told Penny about the ghost sightings, but the Tiki Hut Grill wasn't the right place to be discussing it. Nor did I need Joe Delaney or Charles Paxton to hear about the investigation—at least not before Dolly was able to speak to Joe. Not that I thought they were necessarily involved, but if the killer thought they knew something, he might harm them.

Besides, if I told Penny at work, she would have squealed with joy at my newfound ability, and the whole restaurant would have wondered what was going on. I already wasn't pleased that six others knew—or eight if I included Uncle Harold and Iggy. No doubt, Iggy would blab to Aimee just to show how much he knew.

"Please give Iggy my sympathies," Penny said. "I know he wanted to be green.

I almost chuckled. Penny was such a softy. "I will."

Her mood suddenly brightened. "I have some news."

For a split second, I thought she was going to tell me she and Jaxson had gone out on a date. Penny had the hots for him when they were in high school, and when Jaxson had first returned to Witch's Cove, Penny had instantly swooned.

"What is it?" I asked. And no, I was not holding my breath, hoping she wouldn't say she had shared a drink or a kiss with Jaxson.

She sighed. "Sam and I had a nice talk."

Oh, no. That was worse. I'd been through this with her before. She and her ex-husband had a rather volatile history together. "I hope that was all it was."

She winked. "It might have been a little more. Glinda, he's changed since that incident with his former partner."

Victor. "How has he changed? It's only been a month."

"He stopped taking all that stuff to enhance his physique."

Okay. That was a step in the right direction. "That's good, but hasn't he stopped before?" Penny was so gullible.

"Yes, but he means it this time."

Uh-huh. "Good to know," I said. If we discussed it further, I might say something I'd regret. "Did you hear that Jaxson is back in town?" I had no idea why I brought that up. At least for the next few days, I needed Jaxson to focus on gathering information on those persons of interest and not on some fan girl who would love to go out with him. Since she and her ex-husband might be back together, perhaps she was no longer interested in Jaxson.

"I did. Is he here to stay?"

Why was I the last to hear the news? "I really couldn't say. I know he's working with Drake though."

"I'll stop in the shop and say hi." A couple came into the restaurant and sat in her section. "I better go. I don't need your aunt yelling at me for shirking my duties."

Aunt Fern didn't yell. She calmly told the servers to stop wasting time—like I was doing right now.

Once Penny left, I checked my phone to see if Jaxson had texted me, but he hadn't. Darn. After work, I planned to see if my mom could help with contacting Morgan. Regardless of the outcome, I would then check with Drake and Jaxson to find out if they'd made any progress on tracking down Emma Paxton or if they had found anything on the other two men.

"Glinda?" my aunt called.

I looked over at the cashier's counter. "Yes?"

"Table four is waiting."

Like I said, she wasn't a fan of daydreaming. I wonder if by drinking that pink potion, there had been more than just the one side effect of seeing ghosts.

I rushed over to take their order. Normally, I spent time chatting with the customers, which inevitably would lead them to ask why I was dressed all in pink and wearing a bejeweled pink crown. I would then explain that everyone who worked at the Tiki Hut Grill was required to wear a costume to work, and that we all chose characters we could identify with. Everyone thought it cute that I was Glinda, the Good Witch of the South.

Considering I hadn't told my best friend about trying to help a dead man, I probably should be the Wicked Witch of the West instead. If I had to dress like her, I'd have to wear a black witch's hat, a black gown, and paint my face green. I shivered at that thought. Black was so not my color.

It seemed like forever before three o'clock rolled around, and my shift was over. Before I clocked out, I had to refill the condiments. Once I completed that task, I didn't dawdle since I had people to see and a crime to solve.

As I walked past the cashier's counter to leave, my aunt crooked a finger and motioned me over. She then pointed to the floor at her feet. "Look who's here," she said with a smile.

I leaned over the counter. "Aimee?"

The black cat looked up "Hiya, Glinda."

She looked happy, but I wasn't sure why the cat was there. "You can go upstairs to visit Iggy if you want."

"That's okay. I like being with Fern." Aimee rubbed her head against my aunt's leg, and I swear it was my aunt who purred.

"That's great." I think.

"Where are you off to?" my aunt asked, as if it was totally natural to have a talking cat at her feet.

I couldn't help but wonder what Uncle Harold thought about this new addition. He usually visited my aunt in that very spot most days. "I haven't seen mom in a while, and I wanted to catch up. For some reason, the funeral business takes a hit during the summer, so she hasn't needed me to help out." Not that the residents of Witch's Cove didn't die, but they seem to pass more often when it was a bit colder.

"Tell her I said hello."

I smiled. "I will."

After I changed, it took all of sixty seconds to reach my parents' funeral home. I unlocked the back door and entered. While I understood the need to maintain a chilly temperature, especially near where they kept the dead bodies, I still shivered.

I headed to the funeral home's back office space. Through the slightly open door, I could see that Mom was at her desk. I knocked, and as expected, Toto, barked. I stepped inside, knelt down, and gave the little Cairn Terrier some affection. "You doing okay, boy?"

Toto barked his answer. My mom turned around. "Glinda, I haven't seen you in a while."

"I know. I've been busy. Can we talk?"

She set down her papers and then took off her glasses. "Of course, sweetie."

Toto trotted over to my mom. She leaned over, picked him up, and placed him on her lap. I pulled up a chair. "It's a long story that begins with Iggy."

My mom chuckled. "Doesn't it always? What has he done now?"

Once more I explained how I'd asked for a spell to turn him green, and then how it had gone wrong. "The next thing I knew this ghost appeared in front of me."

"A ghost?"

I had expected that surprised reaction. I calmly explained who Morgan Oliver was and how he'd asked me to help find his murderer. I didn't see the need to discuss my interaction that took place afterward with Steve, Jaxson, or Dolly just yet.

"What can I do to help?" Mom asked.

"Morgan keeps disappearing on me since he doesn't have the energy to take his human form for long. Since I have more questions, I thought maybe you could contact him. He's a real nice guy. I can write down what I want to know if you could ask him for me."

"I would be happy to. Let's go to the conference room where I can spread out."

She handed me a pad and a pencil. My mother gathered some candles, along with her blend of special herbs. After she closed the door on an unhappy dog, we left.

"This place is dead," I said, not intending to make a pun.

"Business has been slow, but I'm actually glad. I thought your dad's health was back to normal, but of late, he's looking pale."

My blood pressure plummeted. "What's wrong?"

"I don't know. He says he's fine, but I don't believe him."

"You need to make him go to the doctor."

Her chuckle was rueful. "That's like trying to convince you to get a real job."

We'd been over that topic many times. Was I living up to my abilities? No. I had a degree in math, but teaching middle schoolers had not been my thing. I loved being with adults and helping them—whether it was serving them food or trying to solve a crime. For now, being a waitress suited me.

We entered the empty conference room. "While I set up, write down your questions," my mom said.

I knew the routine. I scribbled down what I wanted my mother to ask Morgan, and she turned off the lights and then lit some incense, something I don't remember her doing when she tried to contact the deceased deputy.

"When did Morgan die?" Mom asked.

"I don't know exactly. Maybe a week ago."

Once I finished writing my questions, I slid the pad across the table. She studied it, nodded that she understood, and then lit the candles. Only then did she sprinkle the herbs in a clearly defined circle around the candles. "I need to concentrate," she said.

That was my cue to sit quietly. I thought about calling Morgan's name, but this was my mom's show. She mouthed something, closed her eyes, and sat very still. When the candles flickered and the herbs started to move on the table, my body froze. Someone or something was here. I didn't see Morgan, but maybe his spirit had come.

"Did you know you had a twin brother?" my mother asked.

One of the chairs scraped across the floor. Morgan

couldn't move anything, so what had caused that? Were some spirits angry at Morgan?

"Uh-huh. I see. No, no, Glinda met him in person." She opened her eyes, looked straight at me, and mouthed, "What is his name?"

"Trevor Whitehall," I whispered. I personally thought this contact from beyond the grave wasn't nearly as effective as me talking to Morgan outright, but I understood how hard it was for him to appear.

"Trevor Whitehall. No? I understand. Joe? Who is Joe?" My mom looked over at me, her brows raised.

It would take me five minutes to give her all the details. I needed to keep the explanation as brief as possible. "Floyd's neighbor."

"No, wait," my mom said. She slumped against her chair and then blew out a breath. "I'm sorry, Glinda. He left. He also told me that he never wanted to be contacted like that again."

"That doesn't sound like Morgan. He was very cordial when I spoke to him both times before."

"Hmm. Do you think there is another Morgan Oliver?"

"Anything's possible, but an imposter wouldn't know about Joe. I'm betting that Morgan is just frustrated that his killer is at large."

"You're probably right. At least we tried. Now tell me who Joe is."

Not wanting my mom to feel left out, I told her about my discussion with our sheriff, with Morgan's neighbors, the Liberty sheriff, and then with Dolly. Joe's name had been brought up a few times. "Now you're caught up."

"I don't like you snooping around like this. It could be dangerous."

I'd heard that one too many times. "I know. That's why it might be time for me to take some self-defense classes or maybe even learn how to handle a weapon."

"Don't even think about using a gun. I know a girl can never be too careful, but if you carry one, and the other person gets the drop on you, they could take the weapon away and kill you."

She had a point. "At the very least, I'll look into self-defense."

Mom pushed back her chair and stood. "I'd be okay with that."

It was time to go. "I'm going to check with Drake and Jaxson to see what they've learned just as soon as I help you put away these candles."

"Thank you." My mom blew them out, and I then helped gather up a few. "Promise me you'll be careful?" Mom asked. "Asking a lot of questions about a murder can have unforeseen consequences."

"I will be careful," I said.

After we finished, I went next door to the Wine and Cheese Emporium. Thankfully, Drake and Jaxson were both there, though Drake was helping a customer in front while Jaxson was unpacking a crate of wine in the storage room in back.

I knocked on the storage room door and then pushed it open. "Hey there," I said.

Jaxson looked up and smiled. "Hey."

I stepped into the cramped space. "Did you have the

chance to check anyone out?"

"I did. Give me a sec, and I'll tell you all about it." Jaxson finished stacking the bottles. He then motioned that we should talk in the main back room. "You'll never guess what I found out about Emma Paxton."

"What is it?"

Chapter Ten

"FLOYD'S WIFE WAS not in Phoenix when either Floyd or her nephew were killed," Jaxson said.

Knock me over with a huff. "Are you sure?"

"As I've mentioned, I can find anything on a computer. You'd be surprised what is public, but for your own safety, I won't bore you with the details."

"Where was she? Don't tell me Witch's Cove."

"Close by would be my guess, but I can't be sure. Shortly before Floyd died, she flew to Florida and rented a car. I called in a favor from a friend who works with highway surveillance. He spotted her rental car heading this way."

That put a new spin on things. "How long did she rent the car for?"

"She has yet to turn it in."

I had to grab hold of the counter to keep steady. "We know that Floyd was killed by a wolf or wolves. Unless she can turn into one, she couldn't have killed him."

"That's for you to decide. I'm just the muscle, remember?" He flashed me another smile, but clearly, he was more than that.

"You have a brain too. I tend to jump to too many conclusions, and I need a level-headed person around."

He laughed. "You think?"

I did not respond to his comment. "Did you get an address in Phoenix for Emma Paxton? Not that she is there."

Jaxson dug a hand in his pocket and fished out a piece of paper. "I did."

"You are good!"

"Thank you."

"Do you have any idea where in Florida she is staying? I'm going to guess that she's not at Morgan's house in Liberty. Her neighbors would question what she was doing there," I said.

"I won't be able to find her location—at least not legally—but how many hotels are there in Liberty?"

"I suspect not many." My mind spun from one scenario to another. "If Emma had anything to do with Morgan's death, she might not appreciate me digging. Hmm. Decisions, decisions. Is there any way to figure out her financial situation?"

"Are you thinking that if she was desperate for cash, she might try to get the farm by knocking off those who stood to inherit it?"

"Possibly, but that's assuming, she's even mentioned in the will. That is one more reason to find out what Floyd's lawyer is willing to share," I said.

"I will not hack into bank records. Your friend, *Steve*, might be willing to help you with that."

Why was Jaxson always picking on our new sheriff? They'd just met last month. "I might." I needed to change the topic. "Any progress on Floyd's brother, Charles?"

"Not much, other than I found his address. Turn the paper over. It's on the back."

I flipped it over. He lived in Winston, just like Dolly said. "I wonder if Steve has spoken to him?"

Jaxson placed a hand on my wrist. "He might have, but I know you. Please don't visit Charles alone. Okay? We don't know if he had anything to do with either death—or at least with Morgan's."

"I won't." I waved the paper, folded it, and stuffed it in my pocket. "First, I'm going to see what Sandy Vickers has to say about who is next in line to inherit the farm."

"I doubt she'll tell you anything—client confidentiality and all," he said.

"Her client is dead."

"It doesn't matter. Morgan's death is part of an ongoing investigation."

Maybe being around logical Jaxson wasn't a plus. "You never know. Sandy might be willing to give me a hint."

Jaxson chuckled. "What are you going to do? Put a spell on her to get her to talk?"

I smiled. "That's not a bad idea."

"Listen, if Morgan didn't have a will, the farm goes to no one. In that case, Floyd's place will be sold," Jaxson said.

"Ugh." Drake was still with his customer in the front of the store, and I didn't want to disturb him. "I'm going to go. Let me know if you learn anything else."

"Will do and be careful."

I wish everyone didn't treat me like I was going to rush into danger. So what if I often acted first and thought afterward? "Always."

Not wanting to disturb Drake, I left by the beachside entrance and headed over to the law firm of Stallwart, Leggers, and Vickers situated on Bay Way, right next to the Beachside

Gym. It was only about a five-minute walk. While I didn't have an appointment, I hoped they'd let me slip in between clients.

Once I explained to the receptionist what information I needed, she was able to get me in, though she did inform me that Sandy was legally obligated not to divulge any information about a case. I told her I'd ask anyway.

"Hi," I said as I entered her office.

"Glinda, how can I help?" Sandy asked.

Sandy was in her mid-fifties with chin length strawberry blonde hair. Her neatly pressed tailored blue suit and peach blouse looked expensive. "Morgan Oliver, Floyd Paxton's—"

"Nephew. Yes. We've met."

"Good. I am rather upset over his loss." I said, which was kind of true. "Would it be possible to learn who is next in line to inherit Floyd's farm? Is it his wife, or his brother, Charles?"

"I'm afraid I can't disclose that information. As for the wife, do you know where she is?"

Aha. That question was telling. "I do."

Sandy leaned back in her chair. "Where?"

I pulled the address from my pocket and handed it to her. It also had Charles' information on the back. "She lives in Phoenix, though it's possible she's already in town."

"Why do you think that?"

I didn't want to get Jaxson in trouble. "The rumor mill has it that she came here shortly before Floyd died. I believe she still hasn't returned her rental car."

"Interesting. Do you know where she is staying?"

"No. My guess would be in Liberty where Morgan lived. I doubt she'd stay in Witch's Cove."

Sandy nodded. "Too many eyes and ears?"

"Absolutely. Is Emma next in line to inherit the farm then?"

"As I said, I can't say."

She didn't need to. I could read between the lines. I pushed back my chair and stood. "Thank you for taking the time to see me."

"Do me a favor?" Sandy asked.

"Sure."

"I've heard how you helped find Cliff's murderer. If you learn anything about Emma's whereabouts, let me know, okay?"

I smiled. I liked Sandy. "Will do."

Once I left, I decided to visit our illustrious sheriff. He would appreciate knowing that Emma might be in the area. I also wanted to see if I could get him to do a little digging into her financials. Wolves might have killed Floyd, but who was to say someone didn't have a hand in guiding them to his house? Was my imagination out of control? Time would tell.

As I stepped through the front door of the sheriff's office, I realized I probably should have grabbed some cookies from the Tiki Hut as it never hurt to spread some summer love.

"Hey, Pearl," I said with a smile. My gaze lasered straight to Steve's desk—make that his empty desk. Darn. "Sheriff's not here?"

"Oh, he's here. Steve moved into Sheriff Duncan's old office."

Interesting. "Does that mean he's getting a deputy?"

"No news on that yet from the mayor. I hope the council works fast, because my grandson works too hard, and he could use the help."

He was working with Misty Willows over in Liberty. That

constituted help, right? "Is he busy?"

Pearl wiggled her brows. "Not for you, he isn't. Go on back."

I wasn't in the mood for Pearl's matchmaking. As if Steve would ever be interested in a witch. Sure, I might have had a little crush on him when I was trying to convince him I had some magical talents, but ever since Cliff's murderer was brought to justice, I hadn't seen much of him.

I knocked on the closed door. A second later, it opened. "Glinda. This is a surprise. I hope you're here to tell me you figured out who killed Morgan Oliver?"

I laughed. "Right. In two days."

"Well, you are a witch after all."

I wasn't sure if he was teasing or not. "May I come in?"

"Of course." Sheriff Rocker stepped to the side and motioned me in. "What's this about?"

Thankfully, his tone remained light. In fact, he seemed to take pleasure in my crazy theories. Wanting to change his not-so-great perception of me, I inhaled to compose myself as I sat in the chair across from his desk. "Did you know that Emma Paxton was, and still might be, in Florida?"

"I recently learned that."

"Oh."

"What I don't know is her current location. Do you know where she is?"

"No, but I don't think she's here in Witch's Cove. Someone would have noticed her in the last few weeks. I was thinking maybe she's staying near Liberty."

"Misty has been checking, but as of yet, hasn't found her."

Misty, Misty, Misty. They seemed to be chummy. "Good."

"Anything else?" he asked.

The sheriff knew about Joe Delaney, so I saw no reason to mention that I'd spoke with Morgan Oliver again. "Nothing more, though if Emma were to inherit Floyd's farm in the case of Morgan's untimely death, maybe she had a hand in killing him."

Steve huffed out a laugh. "Really? Do you have any proof?"

"No. And that's where I thought you could help."

The sheriff tucked in his chin. "Me, how?"

"Get access to her bank records. If she ran out on Floyd, I doubt she's accumulated a lot of money in the short time she was in Phoenix. She might be desperate for money." Since he didn't interrupt me, I went on. "Apparently, she left Floyd because he had secrets. Learn those, and you might find out who robbed him."

Steve leaned back in his chair. "As a matter of fact, I have investigated her background."

My pulse soared. "And?"

"And, nothing. I'm not at liberty to discuss it. Remember, this is an ongoing investigation."

Sheesh. He sounded like Sheriff Misty Willows and Sandy Vickers. "Fine."

"Anything else I can do for you?" he asked, his lips almost forming a smile.

I doubt he'd tell me, but I had to ask. "Is Charles Paxton a suspect? I heard the two brothers didn't get along."

He picked up his pencil and tapped it on the desk. And

yes, I know he wasn't supposed to tell me anything, but deep down, I had the sense he wasn't ready to dismiss me as a total kook. I brought valuable intel to the table, and he knew it. "I spoke with Charles, but he said he hadn't seen his brother in months."

That wasn't much help. "You believed him?" I asked.

"It doesn't matter if I do or don't. I can do nothing without proof."

That was one nice thing about what I did. No proof needed—just gossip. "Understood. And Joe Delaney? Any proof he was involved?"

"Other than some witnesses claiming he and Floyd's nephew had a shout out, no. Just so you know, Morgan's death is not my jurisdiction," Steve said.

"I know. It's Misty's."

"Yes," he said. When he crossed his arms over his chest, I figured trying to learn anything else was probably futile.

I lifted my chin. "Keep in touch."

His smile came out in full force. "As always."

Before I returned home and was grilled by Iggy, I wanted to do a quick stop at the Spellbound Diner to see if Dolly had learned anything. I also would take advantage of one of her sweet rolls. That and a sweet tea were just what I needed. Today had not been as productive as I'd hoped.

I had to take that back. Jaxson had come through with vital information about Emma. I had met her once a long time ago, and she'd seemed quite timid. Because I was a witch, I had the sense she might tell me things she wouldn't confide in others.

I stepped inside the diner, ready to learn more.

Chapter Eleven

I HADN'T EVEN taken my seat before Dolly rushed past me and slipped into the booth I was about to claim. I slid in across from her.

"I talked with Joe," Dolly spat out without even saying hello.

Excitement surged through me. "What did he say?"

"He said that he and Floyd had been friends and that they'd promised each other not to let any big developers take over either of their farms."

"I didn't know any developers were interested in that area. It's a few miles from the beach. However, if Joe bought Floyd's one-hundred acres and combined it with his spread, it would make that property even more desirable for something—at least in the future."

"I totally agree, which was why I kept pressing him for the real reason he wanted Floyd's place." Dolly leaned back, one brow raised.

Just when I was about to learn something, one of the waitresses rushed over and asked for my order. "I just want a sweet tea and one of those apple pastries. Thanks." The server nodded and headed back to the kitchen. "If Joe was up to no good, I'm surprised he was willing to even talk to you," I said.

Dolly smiled and puffed up the back of her hair, the kind of gesture that implied her seventy-year old sexiness appealed to Joe. She might be right too.

"I'm good at getting people to talk."

That much was true. I've seen it in action a few times. "What else?"

"He finally admitted that his great, great grandfather used to own both parcels of land, but that during the depression he was forced to sell half to the Paxtons. Now that Joe is more financially stable, he wants to reunite the two pieces of land."

"As a tribute to his relatives?"

"Who knows his reasoning."

"Most likely he figured the land would appreciate. Personally, I would have waited until the property went up for sale."

"Exactly," she said. "Which is why I know there is more to the story." She leaned over. "Joe never was a sentimental guy. I don't see him wanting to honor anyone but his own pocketbook."

I chuckled. "I get the sense that Floyd was a little like that too."

"So true. That's why I think you need to find out if maybe his great, great grandfather buried something on Floyd's property. It's the only thing that makes sense. At first, I thought it might be oil, but I think the ground is too shallow for drilling."

Not that one could bury oil, nor did I think there was much in Florida other than in the Gulf waters, but I understood what she meant. And here I thought I had a vivid imagination!

"Maybe he's interested in mineral rights, assuming there are any underground, though I'm not sure if people even own the land below the ground," I said. "If the minerals are below Floyd's one hundred acres, they should be below Joe's as well since the two properties share a border."

"You'd have to ask a lawyer about that. All I know is that Joe wasn't being totally honest with me." She leaned back. "I can tell these things."

The server delivered my iced tea and my pastry. "Thanks." I turned back to Dolly. "That was good sleuthing."

"I loved it. Let me know if you learn anything or need any more help. You know how much I like to dig."

"Will do." That was assuming I wanted all of Witch's Cove to find out about it.

Once Dolly left to tend to things, I sipped on my tea and let my mind race. Steve wouldn't care about this tidbit of information since it was all speculation. Aunt Fern, however, might be able to shed some light on the issue. She was friends with the property record keeper who might be willing to give my aunt the name of this great, great, grandfather. From there, I'd let Jaxson do his magic and search on the Internet for answers. This was shaping up to be quite a mystery. I wasn't so naïve not to consider that his wanting-to-buy-the-property thing had nothing to do with any murder, but I had to try.

I also had to assume that Sheriff Misty Willows had already questioned Joe regarding his whereabouts when Morgan was killed, since she'd been aware of the argument. If Joe had nothing to do with either death, what was his crime? Being a hothead? Ugh. Rabbit holes were not my thing.

After I finished and paid, I returned to the Tiki Hut where Aunt Fern was cashing out someone. When she was finished, I strode up to the counter.

"Glinda, you look excited."

"I guess I am. I need a favor."

My aunt's eyes shone. "Is it about you-know-who?"

I didn't know whether she meant Morgan Oliver, Jaxson, Steve, or Joe Delaney, but I answered anyway. "Yes." I briefly discussed what Dolly had told me. "I thought maybe you could contact Luann over in property records and ask her for the name of Joe Delaney's great, great, grandfather—the one who originally bought the property."

"They'll be closed at this hour."

"I know. I meant tomorrow."

Aunt Fern's eyes sparkled. Like Dolly, she enjoyed uncovering answers. In this case, she probably just wanted to know more than her nemesis. "I will do that first thing tomorrow morning."

A cat meowed, and I leaned over the glass case. "Aimee. Nice to see you again. Have you moved in or something?"

"I've been meaning to tell you," my aunt said, looking a little guilty. "I have asked Aimee to stay with me for as long as she wants."

I really liked that idea. While Uncle Harold kept her company, my aunt couldn't hug him like she could a cat. "I think that's great."

"Really?"

"Absolutely. If Aimee is ever bored, she can visit with Iggy." I leaned over the counter again. "He did apologize for the way he treated you, right?"

"He did. We're all good."

"That's nice to hear. Speaking of Iggy, I'm going to check on him."

After I said goodbye to my aunt, I headed upstairs. As expected, Iggy was on his wicker seat facing the ocean. He didn't even bother turning around when I came in. "What are you mad about this time?" I asked.

"You've been ignoring me."

That was a tired refrain. "I'm not ignoring you. I was trying to find out who will inherit the Paxton farm now that Floyd and Morgan are dead and why Joe Delaney wants Floyd's property so bad."

He swiveled around. "Did you figure it out?"

"Let me get settled, and I'll tell you everything. And yes, I've learned a lot." I stepped into the bedroom to change my top. When I returned to the living room, Iggy was on the sofa, obviously excited to learn more.

I plopped down. "Where did I leave off?"

"Dolly was going to talk to Joe Delaney."

"I'm impressed," I said.

"Why is that?"

"You can keep all of this mess straight even though you hear things second hand."

"That is all the more reason why you should take me with you next time," Iggy said.

I'm not sure I understood his logic. He was doing quite well by staying home. "I did speak with Dolly, but before that, I'd visited with Floyd's lawyer who implied that Emma Paxton is next in line to inherit the farm." Okay, she never came out and said it, but I'd inferred from her question about

Emma, that Floyd's wife was somehow important.

He stretched out on the sofa. "Do you think she killed him?"

"I have no reason to believe so." Unless she was so poor that she felt she had to.

"What else? Did Dolly find out anything interesting?" he asked. It was curious that he dismissed Emma's possible guilt so quickly.

I basically ran through my entire day. "Once Aunt Fern contacts Luann in the property records department, I'll figure out my next step."

"Why don't you ask Gertrude Poole for some help?"

"Why her?" Did Iggy know something that I didn't?

"She's old. As in she's ancient. She might have been around when Mr. Delaney's great, great grandfather bought the farm."

I laughed. "She's only about ninety," I said.

"How old do you think his great, great grandfather would be if he were alive?"

That was an excellent question. "Assuming an average of twenty-five years per generation, the man would have been born in the mid to late eighteen-hundreds."

"Oh. Maybe there was a scandal when she was young that she might remember."

"Like what? Do you think Delaney's father or grandfather murdered ten people and buried them on his property? If so, he wouldn't have sold half the land. Or did he figure they'd never be disturbed?" I asked.

"I don't know, but I don't think there were large back hoes back then or ground penetrating radar to find the bodies.

I think the old man would be safe in thinking he could sell his half, and no one would be the wiser," Iggy said.

I chuckled. I had one smart iguana. "Where did you learn about stuff like that?" Ground penetrating radar, indeed.

"On the Internet. You work a lot. A guy has to stay sharp for the ladies."

"You are a trip, Iggy Goodall."

"Anything else you care to share?"

I'm not sure what more he thought I knew. "When I learn the owner's name, I'll do a deep dive in the library annals. I bet Delilah Smithson could find out what happened back then."

Iggy jumped up and down. "We're really going to do this, aren't we?"

I laughed. "You mean solve the crime?"

"Yes."

"You are right." The two of us were a team. Sounding boards like Iggy played a big role in figuring things out.

IT WASN'T UNTIL after two o'clock the next day that Aunt Fern motioned me over, once I had finished taking an order and giving it to the kitchen. I leaned across the counter. Sure enough, Aimee was there. Poor Uncle Harold. I hope he didn't feel as if he'd been replaced. "Did you speak with Luann?" I asked.

"I did." My aunt pulled out a piece of paper. "Joe Delaney's great, great grandfather was Alan Delaney. He originally purchased all two hundred acres. Then in 1932,

Joe's grandfather, Fred Delaney, sold the land to Dexter Paxton."

"That's good info. After work I'll do a little research."

She smiled. "I have to say, you never look so excited as when you are solving a case."

I chuckled. "I think the math side of my brain likes to be exercised every once in a while."

"Well, if you ever want to start your own sleuthing company, you have my blessing."

My own company? I don't think so. I imagine my parents, as well as Drake, would have a fit. They'd say it was too dangerous, even if all I did was follow spouses around to see what they were up to. "I don't think I want the responsibility. I enjoy waiting on tables."

My aunt dipped her chin. "You are brilliant, Glinda. You need something more fulfilling."

I was convinced that my family would never stop bugging me about finding a better job, but I don't think they would want me running an investigative firm—my aunt being the exception. "I'll keep that in mind."

Not wanting to get into a discussion about my failed life choices again, I spun around and checked on all of my tables. Thankfully, several people came in about then, which kept me quite busy until my shift was over. As much as I wanted to clock out at three on the dot, I waited for my last table to finish before I did. When I'd completed all of my chores, I went upstairs to change out of my outfit. Sparkles and crowns weren't exactly suitable attire for a library—especially one that was always very cold.

Because I had serious work to do, I threw on a pair of

light pink pedal pushers, a dark pink, long sleeved T-shirt, along with my low-cut pink canvas shoes. I was all set.

"Where are you going?" Iggy asked.

"Aunt Fern told me the name of Joe Delaney's relative who purchased the property so long ago, and I want to see if there was any scandal around that time."

Iggy hopped off of his stool. "Take me with you.

"To the library? We can't really talk there."

"That's okay. I just want to get out of the apartment." He looked up at me. "You do realize that if you leave me here, we can't talk either?"

I laughed. "You are right. Okay, you can come, but no crawling around and scaring people, okay?"

"Moi?"

I laughed. I had no idea where he'd learned that French word. I grabbed my larger purse from the bedroom. "Hop in."

Once Iggy was snuggled inside, we took off. While the library was only half a mile away, it was hot out, so I drove. Halfway there, Iggy climbed out of my purse and hung onto the side of the window to look out. He always loved car rides.

When we arrived, I made him get back in my purse. "Remember, you promised to behave."

"I will. Cross my heart."

"Okay then." Inside, the library was cool and quiet—just the way I liked it.

I found Delilah Smithson, the librarian. We'd gone to high school together, and even though I was focused on the sciences, and Delilah devoured English and History, we became friends. I ended up tutoring her in math while she helped me with my history projects. It was a mutually beneficial relationship.

"Glinda, so nice to see you again."

"You too. I have a little project I need to research."

My friend's eyes sparkled. "I love a challenge. How can I help?"

I explained about wanting to learn more about Alan and Fred Delaney. "Anything before 1932 would be good since that was when Delaney sold the land to Mr. Paxton. I know this sounds crazy, but I'm wondering if there is a reason why Joe is so anxious to have Floyd's farm."

"Why the interest?" Delilah asked.

"I had met Floyd's nephew, the one he left his farm to, but he was murdered about a week ago."

"Oh, wow. I'm sorry. Do you think learning why someone bought land almost a hundred years ago will help solve a murder?"

That was an excellent question, but I wasn't about to tell her the dead man's ghost asked me to help. "I have a gut feeling that the property changing hands might still be a bone of contention between the nephew's uncle and the Delaneys."

"Maybe the Delaneys want the land to expand their ranch into farming," she said.

"It's possible, though I will have to see whether Joe actually needs to expand like he is claiming. One hundred acres isn't enough for his cows?"

"I know very little about farming or ranching, but we won't learn anything by guessing. Come with me. The only things that old are on microfiche."

I had been hoping for books, but maybe newspaper articles would be the best. Once Delilah set me up at the station,

I wasn't even sure where to begin. It wasn't as if there was a search function for this stuff. I spent the first hour looking through the events around the time of the Great Depression, but I didn't find much. I was becoming rather frustrated when Delilah showed up with a book.

"Hey. You said you wanted some scandal back when Delaney sold half of his property. I might have found something. Here is a collection of cases on famous bank robbers in our area back in the 1900s. Some thieves were caught. Others were not, but quite a lot of the stolen money was never found. I have no idea if any of this is true, but it's interesting."

"That has potential. Maybe Alan Delaney robbed a bank and buried the money on the land—land that eventually was sold to the Paxtons. Did these bank robbers have names?"

"None that I've found, but the most interesting story happened right here in Witch's Cove."

"Oh, that sounds good," I said. "Tell me about it."

"The robbers were like a Bonnie and Clyde couple, but they were never caught—at least not that I've read about."

"Maybe they didn't get caught because they stashed the loot where no one would look," I said.

Delilah chuckled. "Like on their own property?"

"Hey, two hundred acres is a lot to check out."

"Maybe. I'll keep digging. There have to be other articles on bank robberies. It happened a lot back then. I'll see if towns near here were hit too."

"I appreciate it," I said. If someone did bury stolen money on the Delaney land, Fred Delaney wouldn't have sold the property without digging it up first—assuming he knew about it—and assuming it happened. I slumped in my seat. There were too many loopholes to my theory, but I wouldn't give up.

For the next two hours, I read article after article on local bank robberies, going back to the beginning of the twentieth century. If I'd lived back then, I wouldn't have kept my money in a bank—nor would I have worked at one. Too many people were injured or killed in those heists. As exciting as this prospect was to investigate, I had to be open to the idea that a bank robbery had nothing to do with Morgan's death.

When my stomach grumbled, I knew it was time to head back home. When I picked up my purse, I realized that Iggy had been rather quiet—too quiet for him. I opened it up and froze. He was gone.

This wouldn't be the first time he'd snuck off, so I tried not to panic. Most likely he was bored and decided to look around. "Iggy?" I whispered. "Where are you?"

No answer.

"Is everything okay?" Delilah asked, sneaking up behind me.

I don't remember the last time Delilah ate at the Tiki Hut Grill, but she might never have met Iggy. She certainly wouldn't have known he could talk since she wasn't a witch. "I brought my pet iguana with me, and he's escaped."

I hoped Iggy didn't hear me call him a pet. He hated that designation.

"Oh, no. Does he bite?"

"No."

For the next few minutes, we searched under the tables and between all of the shelves. Just as I was about to give up, the electric front doors opened, and a young boy walked in. To my surprise, Iggy was right behind him. With his head held high, he pranced in.

"Oh, there he is. Thanks again, Delilah, for all your help."

"He went outside?"

I chuckled, trying to make light of the situation. "He'll follow anyone."

I was so going to kill him.

"I enjoyed the search. We need to catch up some time," Delilah said.

"For sure." I then rushed toward the exit working hard not to let my anger get the best of me. "Iggy, where have you been?" I growled.

"I was talking to Gertrude Poole, and I have a lot to tell you."

Since Delilah wasn't far behind me, I pretended not to hear him. I picked him up and placed him in my purse. As quickly as I could, I left. I had so much to say to Iggy, but when I was in this mood, it was better to calm down first.

I placed my purse on the floor of the car and then took off. "Why didn't you tell me you were leaving? I was worried about you."

"Sorry. I didn't want to disturb you," Iggy said. "Besides, it was freezing in the library. You know I don't work well in the cold."

"You're right. I should have packed a small blanket for you."

"I swear, when I left, I planned to bask in the sun for only a few minutes and come right back."

Iggy always had an excuse for everything, though this one

was probably true. "Out of the blue, you remembered that the Psychics Corner was just two blocks down the street, and you couldn't help but see if Gertrude Poole was available. Does that about sum it up?"

He lowered his head. "Yes."

What was done was done. In silence, I drove home, parked, and carried him inside to our apartment. Iggy climbed out and sat on the sofa.

"I'm going to fix myself something to eat," I said. "I'm hungry."

"Fix me some arugula if you don't mind."

How could he be so calm? He could have been hurt running around, but he'd never understand that.

I shoved yesterday's leftovers in the microwave and poured a sweet tea. While it was cooking, I placed some lettuce leaves and arugula on a plate and carried it out to Iggy.

"Thank you," Iggy said as polite as could be.

After my meal was finished heating, I grabbed the plate and my tea, and returned to the living room. "Spill," I said.

Chapter Twelve

"I WILL ADMIT that walking the two blocks from the library to the Psychics Corner was quite a journey, especially since some kid on a bike almost ran me over," Iggy explained.

I worked hard not to say anything about how dangerous it was for someone so small to be out and about. Thank goodness for his rather shiny, pink diamond-studded collar. It acted as a kind of reflector. "Go on."

"With a little sweet talking, I was able to get in to see Gertrude. She is wonderful, by the way, even if she is more ancient than sin."

"Be nice. In her day, Gertrude Poole was our most powerful witch in town," I said.

"She's not now? What happened?"

"According to rumor, after doing so many spells, she decided to retire and just do psychic readings."

"I'll keep that in mind the next time I see her," Iggy said.

I didn't tell him there wouldn't be a next time. "What did you ask her?"

"I said you and I were investigating the death of Morgan Oliver as well as the break-in at his uncle's house."

That wasn't a question. And we weren't exactly looking into the break-in. Just the murder. "Did she even know that

Floyd Paxton was dead?"

"She did. After a lengthy back and forth, she revealed she had performed a spell on two garnet necklaces for Floyd not long ago."

I liked the sound of that. "What kind of spell?"

"Considering Floyd was dead, she was willing to reveal that the spell was to prevent him from harming others."

I wondered if it was some kind of anger management inhibitor. "Interesting. Did she say why he needed two necklaces." And why a necklace? I couldn't imagine him wearing it.

"No." Iggy dipped his head and munched on the lettuce. From the speed with which he was eating, he was as hungry as I was.

I polished off my meal in no time, my mind going in a hundred different directions. "I'm going to talk with Drake and Jaxson about your findings. They might have a different spin on it."

Tomorrow, I might drop in on Gertrude and probe a bit deeper. She wouldn't have come out of retirement unless it was for a very good reason. Floyd Paxton was a dour old farmer, but I'd never heard that he was violent—other than from Miriam who thought Floyd killed his wife. We now know, that wasn't true.

The best person to ask about that would be Emma. Unfortunately, she was eluding everyone's notice.

Iggy looked up. "I did good, right?"

I did not correct his grammar even though I wanted to. "You did. What role these magical necklaces played, if any, in Morgan's death, I don't know, but Floyd must have wanted them a lot if he was willing to meet with a psychic." Not everyone in Witch's Cove believed in them. "Before I speak with the Harrison brothers though, I want to see if the sheriff found those necklaces at Floyd's house."

"That would be a good start," Iggy said. "If they were valuable, and they are missing, it could have been what was stolen."

"My thoughts exactly. Oh, I think Aimee has moved in with Aunt Fern."

He spun around. "I know."

I enjoyed seeing my familiar happy for a change. I left by the main entrance since I'd heard Aunt Fern come up the stairs already. I crossed the street and entered the sheriff's department.

Pearl looked up and smiled. "Glinda, this is getting to be a regular occurrence."

I laughed, because I didn't want her to think I was interested in the sheriff. "I thought you got off work at six."

"Jennifer, the late-night person called in sick. Actually, one of her ten-year old twins is really ill. But don't worry. Steve is insisting that I leave by nine." Pearl smiled.

"Being short-handed isn't fun. If Penny is out for any reason, it is tough on all of us. Is the sheriff available?" I didn't need to be gossiping when I had work to do.

"He is. Go on back. Just knock on his door."

I wondered when the poor man rested. He couldn't be on call twenty-four hours a day. I probably should have waited until tomorrow to tell him about the necklaces, but I wanted to figured things out as quickly as possible.

I hoped he didn't think my question about some magical

jewelry was stupid, and that I was wasting his time. I just wanted to know if the necklaces were anywhere around when the cops searched the house after Floyd died. I knocked on Steve's closed office door.

"Come in."

I entered and smiled. "Hi."

I expected Steve to be annoyed with me stopping in, especially at this hour, since I had a tendency to make some pretty bold statements, but he merely leaned back and returned my smile. "To what do I owe the pleasure?"

I sat down in the chair facing his desk. "There is a slim possibility that I figured out what might have been stolen from Floyd Paxton's house."

Steve sat up. "Really? What?"

"I chatted with Gertrude Poole a while ago."

"Poole? Ah, yes, didn't you say she was a psychic?"

Darn. Maybe I shouldn't have given my source, but it was too late now. "Yes, but I didn't go for a psychic reading." Actually, I personally didn't go at all, but there was no way I could convince him that my iguana could talk. "I asked her what she knew about Floyd's break-in."

"Why would she know anything about that? From what I've been able to deduce, he wasn't the witchy type."

"He wasn't, which makes what I'm about to tell you all the more interesting. Apparently, he went to her because he wanted her to put a spell on two garnet necklaces that he had."

"A spell? What kind?"

"The spell was to prevent him from harming others."

Steve placed a palm over his mouth and then dragged it

down his chin. "I don't remember hearing that he was dangerous."

"Me neither, but Miriam thinks he might have killed Emma and buried her on his property, remember?"

"Ah, yes. I said we didn't have the manpower to search on his land."

"Exactly. I thought I might ask Miriam again about him to see what light she can shed on the situation."

"Good idea. Do that. I, too, heard a rumor," he said.

This was interesting. "About?"

"That Emma Paxton left because Floyd had harmed her."

"I'm not sure it's the truth. I'd love to meet with her and ask her about it," I said.

"Me too." He leaned forward. "I've been looking for Floyd's wife, as has Misty, but to no avail. If anyone mentions her whereabouts, let me know. She must have had some friends in town."

My pulse shot up. Steve Rocker was actually asking for my help. "Sure. I'll try."

I probably should at least mention my theory about why Joe wanted to buy Floyd's property, but I wanted to have a few more facts before I did. I pushed back my chair and stood. "I'll let you know if I learn anything."

"Thank you, Glinda. It's helpful when the town folk pitch in."

I was just one of the many town folk now? Interesting. To be honest, I didn't know what I wanted to be in his eyes, other than someone who brought value to the table.

I left the department and headed over to the wine and cheese shop, hoping one of the Harrison brothers was there. I stepped inside and the bell above the door chimed. "Hello?" I called out.

A second later, Drake came in from the back. "Hey!"

I was happy to have the chance to chat with him. "Got a sec?"

"Sure."

I gave him a rundown of what I'd learned since the last time I'd seen him. "What do you think?" I asked.

"It still seems as if there might be two different crimes here—or rather four."

Four. Was he talking about Floyd being mauled as one of them? No one should blame an animal for doing what came naturally. "I assume you mean three: the two break-ins and Morgan's murder."

"Yes. Three. Your bank robbery idea isn't half bad, but your timeline might be off," Drake said.

"How so?"

"I'd go back further in time to the great grandfather maybe. I'm thinking closer to 1900 rather than 1932. Then do your spreadsheet thing."

"That's an excellent idea." I think. I wasn't sure of his logic, but I was game to check it out. Thankfully, Delilah's book dated back to 1900. "In regard to the spell put on two garnet necklaces, I plan to speak with Gertrude tomorrow. Iggy didn't ask enough questions."

Drake smiled. "He is something else, isn't he?"

"If you mean he disregards danger, then yes."

Drake laughed. "Sounds like someone else I know."

He might be right. The bell above the door chimed, and another customer entered. "I'll let you go, but if anyone mentions Emma, try to find out if they have any idea where she might be staying. I'm thinking she's closer to Liberty than here."

"Will do."

Drake greeted his customer, and I hoofed it back to the Tiki Hut Grill. The five gossip queens needed to prove their worth. If anyone could find Emma, they could—and that included Steve's grandmother, Pearl.

My job for the evening was to create that spreadsheet like Drake suggested. Not that I planned digging up the property, but wouldn't it be great if we caught Joe in the act? Was it a long shot? Absolutely, but Iggy always was saying that I needed to think big.

I'd no sooner stepped into my apartment, when my phone rang. It was Delilah. "Hey, there," I said. "Did you find something?" It was the only reason I could think of why she'd be calling so soon.

"I did. I was able to access the courthouse public records. I went back as far as 1900. I searched for any kind of robberies, from banks to jewelry stores to high-end homes."

Delilah was smart. "I hadn't thought of that. Good job," I said.

"Thanks. Anyway, one—or rather two names—popped up. Apparently, we had a local Bonnie and Clyde right here in Witch's Cove."

My pulse skyrocketed. "Do you have names or dates?"

She giggled. "Yes, and you won't believe who they were."

She was killing me. "Who?"

"Mary and James Delaney."

My knees buckled, and if I hadn't been standing next to

the sofa, I might have ended up on the floor. "Tell me more."

"Okay. In 1904, a Tampa bank was robbed, but the thieves were never caught."

I'd read about a lot of cases where the thieves escaped. "How does that relate to Witch's Cove?"

"Just wait," Delilah said. "There were ten more bank robberies all up and down the west coast of Florida in the next few years. Mary and James Delaney weren't caught until…get this, 1909 once they were found to be connected to ten of them."

"Wow. All those years of robbing banks meant a lot of money." I didn't want to jump to any conclusions about whether or not these two were related to Joe Delaney. There also didn't seem to be any information that showed they'd buried the money on the Delaney property either. "Where were they caught?"

"Right here in Witch's Cove. They actually died in a shootout trying to rob one of our banks."

Darn. "That meant they didn't spill the beans about what they did with the money from all of the other robberies."

"No, which means it could be anywhere," Delilah said.

"You have been a huge help."

"I love researching. Please don't hesitate to call on me again."

"I won't."

I disconnected and leaned back against the sofa. Iggy jumped onto my lap. "Tell me, tell me."

I went through what she'd found out. "That doesn't mean there is buried treasure on Floyd's property," I warned.

"No, but there could be. Who would know?" Iggy asked.

"Besides the thieves? I doubt Floyd or Emma would know. If they had a map to the location of the money, they would have dug up their place already. I'm not about to ask Joe either. If it is true there is money there, that could put us in danger if he thinks we know."

Iggy's eyes widened. "Why?"

"Bad people like to hurt family members."

He jumped off my lap. "What do we do?"

"I would like confirmation that Mary and James Delaney are related to Joe."

"How are you going to find that out?" Iggy asked.

"Why Dolly Andrews, of course. Aunt Fern said she's into genealogy. I bet she'd know how to trace a family tree."

"Can I come with you?"

I laughed. It was around dinner time. Dolly might work the night shift on a Friday night. Since I'd eaten, I wouldn't order much. "Sure."

My pink iguana was a good sport, and at times, he had really good ideas.

Chapter Thirteen

I WASN'T SURE if Dolly would be at the diner or not, but I had to at least check. I hadn't paid attention to her personal hours, but if she wasn't there, I wouldn't mind a hot fudge sundae as consolation. Who am I kidding? I wanted a dessert even if she was there.

When I stepped inside, I blew out a breath.

"Is she here?" Iggy asked from inside my purse.

"Yes."

"Oh, goodie."

I was lucky to have an iguana who was just as interested as I was in this crime solving stuff. I checked out the crowd. Good for Dolly. The Spellbound Diner was definitely busy this time of night. I considered myself lucky to snag the last remaining booth.

As soon as Dolly delivered a hamburger and a grilled chicken sandwich to one of the tables, she rushed over. "Will you be dining or chatting?" She winked.

Dolly lived for gossip. "Both, as a matter of fact."

"Ooh. Sounds good. What will you have?"

"I'll have the chocolate sundae and a sweet tea." I opened my purse so she could see Iggy. "How about one lettuce leaf for my buddy here?"

Dolly smiled. "You got it."

A few minutes later, she delivered the food and slid in across from me. "I'm kind of short-handed," she said apologetically. "I only have a few minutes."

"I'll be quick. I learned there was a series of bank robberies in this area in the early 1900s. The criminals? Mary and James Delaney."

As I'd hoped, she sucked in a breath. "Are they related to you-know-who?"

I chuckled. If anyone had been listening, they would have known who she was talking about. "That's what I'd like your help with. Aunt Fern said you are a whiz at this family tree stuff."

Her chin tucked under. "Fern said that?"

"Yes, you have quite the reputation." It never hurt to butter her up, especially when it was true.

"Oh, my. I'd be happy to take a look, but I could just ask Joe."

I inhaled. "I thought of that, but doing so might tip him off that we are looking into his background. Even if he is innocent of everything, I couldn't tell you the names of any of my relatives from way back then."

"I could, but that's me. I'll do a little research and let you know."

I dipped my spoon into the ice cream and chocolate sauce. At the first taste, I groaned. "This is divine."

"Thanks. Have you learned anything else?" she asked, clearly not interested in my food critique.

I plucked the lettuce from the plate and fed it to Iggy. If his mouth was full, Iggy wouldn't be able to mention his visit to Gertrude Poole. I didn't need Dolly to talk that up, since it would be hard enough to keep Joe Delaney from learning about my investigation. "Not yet."

She smiled. "I need to get to work, but I'll let you know what I find out about the family tree."

"Thanks. I just need to see if they were related to Joe's family lineage. Even if they are, there is no guarantee they buried their bank take on his land."

She smiled. "I know, but it will be fun to learn about this exciting rogue couple."

I chuckled. "For sure."

After I finished the dessert and chased it down with a tea, Iggy and I headed out. We'd done enough damage for the day. It was time for a relaxing glass of wine and some mindless TV.

I had no sooner settled in for the night when Aimee shot through the cat door. Part of me wanted to ask her to knock first until I realized that was physically impossible. When someone knocked a few seconds later, I jumped. "Yes?"

The door opened, and Aunt Fern stepped inside. It might be time to use the lock on the door. Not that I minded her coming and going whenever she wanted, but anyone from the restaurant could have climbed the stairs and entered.

My aunt looked around. "Where's Iggy?"

I was just about to say he was in the kitchen when the little fellow came waddling out. "I'm here." He stopped. "Aimee! Nice to see you."

I was about to suggest that they chat in my bedroom where it would be quieter and more private, but Aimee all but ignored my iguana and wrapped her tail about Aunt Fern's legs instead. Typical cat.

"Have a seat," I said. "Can I get you some hot tea?"

It didn't matter what the temperature was outside, my aunt loved her tea.

"I'm good, dear. I have news."

My aunt plopped down on the sofa, and Aimee jumped up next to her. My aunt really seemed to be an animal whisperer since I never met an animal who didn't love her.

I waited to hear what she had to say, but she just smiled with her lips together. "Tell me," I begged.

"I found Emma Paxton."

I sucked in a breath. "You did?"

"Yes, or rather a friend of mine who lives on the outskirts of Liberty found her," Aunt Fern said.

"Where is she?"

My aunt shoved a hand in her apron pocket and withdrew a piece of paper. "She's renting an apartment outside of Liberty—under an assumed name, mind you."

I bet that was why neither Misty Willows nor Steve could locate her. "That's great news."

"Are you going to tell Steve about your find?" she asked.

I wasn't able to tell whether she wanted me to or not. "Probably, but I'd like to speak with Emma first. And don't worry. I'll ask either Drake or Jaxson to go with me. I'm not so naïve to think that she is automatically innocent. Unless she can turn into a claw scratching animal though, I doubt she killed her husband."

Aunt Fern laughed. "I would like to see that—at a distance, of course. Just make sure not to turn your back on her."

"What, you think she plans to shoot me? She barely

knows me."

"Just saying."

My aunt was too paranoid.

Aimee arched her back. "I think it's possible that she could change into an animal. I mean, if I can talk—which means I'm part human—why can't a human be part cat?"

Or wolf as the case may be. "That's an excellent question, Aimee. I'll try to keep an open mind."

We chatted a bit more, but Iggy kept butting in. I could tell he was just trying to get Aimee's attention, but she wasn't having any of it. I felt sorry for him since he sincerely believed that he and Aimee were meant to be.

After a bit of catching up, Aunt Fern and Aimee left. As much as I enjoyed chatting, I felt drained and lifted myself off the couch. "I'm heading to bed. I have a full shift tomorrow."

"You should quit. Working is cutting into your investigation time."

I laughed. "Life doesn't work that way. Goodnight."

"Night."

Once I snuggled into bed, I picked up a book, but my mind refused to focus. I had to speak with Gertrude and then Emma tomorrow. If only I knew what to say, I wouldn't be so nervous.

AS USUAL, SATURDAYS were very busy. People loved going to the beach during the glorious days of summer and then grabbing lunch. The one good thing about working was that it gave me time to figure out what I wanted to say to Gertrude.

She would probably repeat what she said to Iggy—that Floyd feared he'd hurt someone, but I thought I'd first check with Maude Daniels to see what they knew about him. Something didn't seem right about Floyd seeking out a witch for his anger management issues.

Penny touched my arm. "I'm going to pick up Tommy from Sam's right now. Do you need me to help with the condiments?"

"No. Go."

She smiled. "I've seen you with Jaxson. How's that going?" Her brows rose.

I didn't know which was worse: people teasing me about Sheriff Rocker or Jaxson Harrison, the bad boy. "Good, though we're just friends."

"Ah, yes, the lie all women in lust say." Her gaze swept to the ceiling.

"Uh-huh. I'll catch you up on Monday, okay?" I had tomorrow off, thank goodness.

"You promise? I miss our chats."

Guilt assaulted me. "Me too, and yes we will talk."

She hugged me and then left. I finished topping off the condiments and headed upstairs. I was just a little stressed. I planned to hit up Maude at the Moon Bay Tea Shop first. She'd mentioned Floyd right after he was killed.

After I changed and told Iggy he couldn't come since I had many stops, I walked one block to the tea shop, happy I would be enjoying one of Maude's amazing ice tea blends. Wanting to support our local merchants, it was my obligation to buy a pastry, right?

I ordered my food and picked my usual table in the corner. A minute later, Maude came over with my food. "Glinda, it's always nice to see you. I hear you are investigating the break-in over at Floyd's place."

Actually, it was Morgan's murder. "Have you been chatting with Dolly?"

"Dolly? No, Miriam."

How did her sister know? Of course. My aunt. "I am. Actually, I wanted to ask you about Floyd. Other than maybe taking out some aggression on his wife, Emma, was Floyd ever violent with anyone?"

"Violent? No. He was a bit withdrawn and not the friendliest man, but I personally never saw him be mean or anything. In fact, it was around last Christmas, when a family from out of town came in. The mom, who had a toddler and newborn, looked really stressed. She ordered some hot chocolate for her son and some milk for the baby that I offered to heat up. I think she only had water. Her situation must have been quite dire, because when she went to pay, she had to dig in her purse for loose change."

"Did Floyd help in some way?" If not, why tell the story?

"As a matter of fact, I saw him ease on up to the counter and drop a ten-dollar bill on the ground. He then tapped her on the shoulder and asked if she'd dropped it." Maude smiled. "You should have seen the look on that mother's face. It was the best. She picked it up, paid for her meal, and handed him the change."

My heart melted. "Aw. I bet Floyd didn't take it, did he?"

"He told her to keep it. He then paid for what he'd ordered and left."

"That doesn't seem like the kind of man who goes around

beating up people."

"No. Why do you ask? It wasn't like he got in a fight and was killed. An animal attacked him."

"I know, but something seems off to me." Otherwise, why would her sister think he'd killed his wife?

"About what? The medical examiner said there were claw marks on his body. He was definitely killed by a wolf. No doubt about it. The animal didn't get away unscathed though, because Floyd had blood under his nails."

"Interesting. I didn't know a man's nails were long enough to dig into the hard hide of a wolf."

"Me neither," she said.

"I heard the sheriff is still trying to find out who robbed poor Floyd. He'll figure it out eventually," I said.

Apparently, Maude didn't know anything more. She pushed back her chair and said her goodbye. Her little story about how kind Floyd had been only added to the mystery. He must have been desperate for that protection spell for some other reason. What could it be though? Since Emma was alive, he didn't kill his wife. I could only hope my conversation with her would provide me with some answers.

After I finished my delicious tea and chocolate scone, I headed over to the Psychics Corner. I probably should have called ahead and made an appointment with Gertrude, but sometimes an impromptu visit was best.

I only had to wait ten minutes before Gertrude finished with her client. When our resident psychic stepped out of her office and saw me, her brow rose in surprise. "Glinda! Did you bring your adorable familiar with you?"

"No, Iggy is minding the store." That was an expression I

figured she'd understand, considering her age. "Do you have a few minutes?"

"Is it about Floyd?"

I nodded. "Iggy wasn't the best at relaying what you said."

Her whole demeanor softened. "I understand. Come in."

Her space was small but cozy. Not only were there pots brimming with blooming flowers under the window, pink and white gingham checkered drapes hung on either side to make it picture perfect. Her two overstuffed leather chairs, together with a hard-backed chair, were separated by a coffee table laden with cookies. No wonder she had a good business. The cookies alone might be worth the fee. "You've spruced up the place since the last time I was in here."

"Oh, that was months ago. You need to stop by more."

I smiled. "I will. Maude told me an interesting story about Floyd a few minutes ago." I detailed his generosity with the woman and her two children.

"That doesn't surprise me," Gertrude said.

"No? Why is that? I thought Floyd wanted a spell that would stop him from hurting others."

"He did," she said.

I waited for her to add something, but when she didn't, it appeared as if Gertrude didn't want to be more forthcoming. "Can you tell me why he wanted the spell put on two necklaces instead of one? Was one for Emma? I never heard she had any violent tendencies." Personally, I didn't see a rugged farmer like Floyd wearing any kind of jewelry, let alone a garnet necklace.

"Floyd was fighting demons—inner ones. It was why he went on a kind of self-retreat every month. I promised Floyd that I wouldn't reveal his secret."

His secret? My palms started to sweat. I wish I knew what to make of this. "Floyd is dead. He can't hurt you now."

Gertrude intertwined her wrinkled hands and smiled. "Secrets often involve more than one person. You might want to ask Emma or his brother. They might be able to shed some light on his issues. But if you do, be forewarned that it could be dangerous for you. Very dangerous."

What did that mean? Up until this point, I wasn't scared, but I was now. "Witch to witch, can you tell me what was special about the garnet necklace? Why not a ring—something that Floyd wouldn't mind wearing? Or didn't he have to actually wear it?" I had no idea why this whole necklace thing bothered me so much.

"As you know, spells by themselves need something to attach themselves to for long lasting effects."

"Yes, I did know that. Garnet jewels are quite hefty, which means—"

She smiled. "I see you understand."

I assumed that meant a strong spell needed to be attached to a really big object. I asked her a few more questions, but that was all I was able to worm out of Gertrude today.

I stood and then held out a hand. "Thank you for your help. Don't get up. I'll pay on my way out."

"Nonsense. Ever since I performed the spell, it has been weighing on me. At the time, I felt I did what was best. This bit of advice is on the house."

More with the cryptic stuff. "I appreciate it."

"Now, if you want a little psychic reading, I'd be happy to charge you—at a witch-to-witch discount, of course." She grinned.

I chuckled. "I may take you up on it one day."

Or not. I didn't need a psychic. I didn't want to know if I would end up a spinster or have a wonderful life with a man. I liked Steve Rocker, but I also liked Jaxson Harrison. Not only that, I was completely devoted to Drake, even though he had no interest in me.

As for learning about other aspects of my future, I didn't want to know if something might happen to Aunt Fern or my parents or Iggy. Nope. I'd rather not know anything until I lived it.

After I left, I almost wished I hadn't come. Gertrude's words were unsettling. I thought she'd tell me about Floyd's inability to handle his liquor or something, not talk about inner demons. Emma had left a few months before he'd asked for the spell. Maybe his regrets were what was driving him to anger.

Darn. I should have left well enough alone. As soon as I had that thought, I could almost hear Drake laugh. He was right. I probably needed help in the meddling department—but not before I spoke with Emma.

With her address in my hand, I set off for the outskirts of Liberty. Before I was even out of Witch's Cove, I remembered that I'd promised Aunt Fern I wouldn't visit Emma by myself, so I pulled over and called Drake.

"Glinda, what's up?" he asked. Voices sounded in the background, which meant he had customers. It made sense since Saturday was his busiest day.

"You're busy. I don't want to bother you. I'm on my way to speak with Emma. I'll just text you her address, so someone knows where I am."

"Oh, no you don't," Drake said. "We don't know anything about her," he whispered. "Where are you?"

"I'm in my car." I gave him the cross streets.

"Stay right there. Jaxson will be there in five."

I sighed. "I don't need a babysitter."

"I know, but if you do, I won't have to worry," Drake said.

Drake was the best. "Fine, but I'll turn around and pick up Jaxson in front of your store. It will only take a minute."

"Perfect." He then disconnected.

I shook my head and smiled. I really loved small towns and how much everyone cared for one another. On the other hand, it kind of drove me crazy that nothing escaped anyone's notice. If anyone saw Jaxson get in my car, tongues would wag. Ah, yes. Life in Witch's Cove was grand.

Chapter Fourteen

JAXSON SLID INTO the passenger seat. "I'm glad you called. I was quite bored."

"You can't fool me. You like working with your brother," I said.

"Correction. I like being with my brother—not working for him. Are you aware he is a slave driver?"

I laughed. "Sure, he is."

"Tell me what you've learned this afternoon. You got off work two hours ago. Surely, you've almost solved the crime of who killed Morgan Oliver."

"Funny man." If anyone had told me in May that I would enjoy spending time with Jaxson a month later, I would have said he was crazy. Ever since his criminal record had been expunged, he'd become a new man.

"You must have been productive," he said.

"You're right. I was." I discussed what Delilah told me about Mary and James Delaney, and then how I asked Dolly to find out if these two bank robbers were related to Joe.

"Since they were from Witch's Cove, I'd say it was highly likely they are relatives," he said.

"That was my thought, but I wanted Dolly to make sure first. Besides, it will keep her out of trouble."

He smiled. "Ah yes. To keep the gossip queens from spreading rumors, you think that if they are busy, they won't have time for much communication."

Jaxson saw right through me. "Guilty, though they all had good information." Next, I told him about Floyd's good deed last Christmas and then what Gertrude said. "She was not telling me everything, which is why I want to speak with Emma."

"Makes sense. Do you think Emma will know about the necklace?"

"I don't know. She arrived back in town a couple of days before Floyd was killed, but that doesn't mean she was at his house on the day of his demise. I think she's been staying at this address since then."

He looked at the paper and entered it into his mobile app to make it easy to find. "What if she won't talk to you?"

"I'll thank her and then contact Trevor to see if he can help us with Morgan staying in his human form."

Jaxson leaned back in the seat. "Trevor, yes. Good idea."

"If Emma doesn't know much, we'll find Morgan. If anyone knows about the necklace and its spell, it would be him."

"Let's see what Floyd's wife has to say."

The trip took about thirty minutes. Her apartment was part of a quadplex. Each building was small and looked more functional than attractive. If I didn't have free rent, no telling what my living conditions might have been.

There was one car in the dirt lot in front of the buildings, but I had no way of knowing who it belonged to. "What apartment number is it?" I asked.

Jaxson checked the paper. "Unit 3."

We both got out. Now I was glad that I'd asked him to come with me. This neighborhood wasn't the best. I knocked on the door, and while I heard someone inside, no one answered.

I rapped on the door again. "Emma Paxton? It's Glinda from Witch's Cove. Can we talk?"

Most likely, she didn't answer because she thought it might have been the police. The door eased open a few seconds later. I had met her one time, but to be honest, I didn't recognize her. Her hair wasn't combed, she wore no makeup, and it appeared as if she'd been crying.

"Yes?" she asked, followed by a sniffle.

I might as well blurt out my connection to the case. "I doubt you'll believe me, but since I'm a witch, I can see ghosts. Your nephew, Morgan, appeared to me and asked if I would help find his killer." I crossed my fingers that she hadn't been the one to pull the trigger. "I could really use your help."

It was as if I'd just handed her a check for a million dollars. "Yes, yes, come in."

While she welcomed us inside, I doubted she fully understood what I'd said. Who lets in someone claiming to have seen a ghost?

The inside was dark and brown. It was an efficiency, with an unmade bed on one wall and a rather messy kitchen on another. Not that the farm she shared with Floyd was a mansion, but it was a sight better than this place.

"This is Jaxson Harrison." Her eyes widened at the name.

She took a step backward. "Weren't you the one who was

involved in the liquor store robbery?"

I held out my hand, hoping Jaxson wouldn't say something we'd both regret. "He was, but he's been cleared of all charges," I said. "Sheriff Duncan announced it last month."

Thankfully, what appeared to be fear in her eyes subsided.

"Oh. I'm happy for you." She motioned to the small table with the four chairs cramped around it. "How do you think I can help?"

Emma barely knew me, but I didn't want her to think we were there to dig up any dirt on her—unless she really had killed Morgan. "Shortly before your husband was taken from us, he visited a psychic."

"Gertrude Poole. He told me when I returned from Arizona."

I thought it best to lay all of my cards on the table. "I know that Floyd asked Gertrude to put a spell on two garnet necklaces to keep him from hurting people."

"He told me that too."

I waited for her to continue, but she did not. "Was Floyd violent?" I asked.

She looked down at her hands that she'd laced together. "Not really. I mean if he drank, he had a temper, but it wasn't like he went out looking for trouble. Floyd was a homebody."

"Then why did he need the spell?"

Emma blew out a breath. "I honestly don't know. He wouldn't tell me anything, regardless of how much I pressed him on it. All I know is that Floyd had issues."

That matched what Gertrude had said.

"What kind of issues?" Jaxson asked. "I mean we are all fighting demons in one way or another."

That was a cool way to slip that into the conversation. It was possible he was referring to himself.

"I wish I knew. He kept secrets from me for sure. Every month he'd leave for a day or two. When he returned, he was like his old self."

"Did he say where he went?" I asked.

"He wouldn't tell me other than to say he needed to clear his head."

If I had that much trouble, I wouldn't think once a month would be enough. "What about his brother, Charles?"

"They didn't get along," she said. "During our marriage, I don't think I saw Charles more than three times."

That was a shame. "Do you know what caused the rift?"

"No, but what does my husband's relationship with his brother have to do with Morgan's death?"

I guess I needed to take a different tactic. "It might not. I've been trying to figure out why someone would shoot Morgan in the back like that. I figured this person either wanted to be the next in line to inherit the farm or thought Morgan knew where those magic necklaces were hidden. It was equally possible he believed Morgan knew the secret about Floyd—a secret that shouldn't get out." I was pretty proud of myself for figuring out that much.

Emma's mouth opened a bit. "I have no idea where the necklaces are, nor did I ever see them. As for your theory about someone not wanting Morgan to reveal my husband's secret, I don't know who that would be. While I am next in line to inherit the farm, I don't want the place even though it was my home for a while. Why would I? I can't keep it up by myself."

"You could sell it," Jaxson said. "I imagine some big developer would love to scoop up one hundred acres around here."

She sucked in a breath. "That might be, but I would never do that. The land has been in Floyd's family for a long time. I would only sell to another farmer."

"Like Joe Delaney?" I asked.

She shrugged. "I'm not sure. Floyd told me that Joe approached him, but that he didn't want to sell to him. He never told me why."

Excitement at a possible break-through built inside of me. "Did Joe state why he was so anxious to buy it? I know he also asked Morgan after your husband passed. The next day Morgan was dead."

Her gaze darted right and then left. "No."

"Why did you really leave Witch's Cove, Mrs. Paxton?" Jaxson asked. That question came out of left field.

I held my breath. I had the feeling that question would not be well received.

"Does it matter?" she asked.

I wanted to reach out and clasp her hand to reassure her, but I sensed she wouldn't have liked it. "It could. I think your husband was hiding something. That something might have been what killed him."

"An animal killed him," she said.

"That's true." However, I had a feeling that a person guided the wolf to Floyd. And no, I had no proof.

She sniffled. "Floyd and I had our differences, mostly because he kept everything to himself. I left because I wanted a man who loved me enough to trust me with all of his concerns."

"Don't we all." If she didn't know what her husband was hiding, nor where the necklaces were, I didn't think she could help us anymore. "Thank you for talking with us."

"Are you going to tell the cops where I am?"

"I won't say anything, but if we found you, they won't be far behind. You might want to give Sandy Vickers a call. She needs to speak with you."

This time, she reached out and cupped my hand. "Thank you, and I will contact our lawyer."

I figured if she was guilty, she'd move tonight. Right now, I wasn't in the mood to keep watch on her. "I guess you're going to put the farm up for sale then?" I asked.

"In due time."

"What about Charles? Would he want the farm?" It was possible, he'd be in line to inherit it if he was Floyd's brother.

"I don't know, but even if he did, that would be a hard no. Now if you would excuse me, I need to go to the store for some food."

That was lame, but she had taken the time to talk to us. I wish Penny had been with us, since she was so good knowing if a person was lying. Sure, she'd goofed with the deputy's killer, but I hoped that was a one-time event. For now, I chose to believe Emma. "In case you think of something, let's exchange phone numbers."

She hesitated but then gave in.

With her phone number stored on my phone, Jaxson and I thanked her again and left. Once in the car, I asked for his take.

"It's hard to say. She seems fairly clueless about what her

husband was up to. If my spouse left every month for some retreat, I might be tempted to follow her."

I chuckled. "That makes two of us. I wonder if Charles knows something."

"Why would he?" Jaxson asked. "Those two didn't get along."

"I know, but something bothers me. I just can't figure out what it is."

"Tomorrow is my day off. What do you say we try to contact Trevor? If he can help keep Morgan up and running for longer than a minute, it could be very helpful," Jaxson said.

"I have off tomorrow too, and that's a great idea. If anyone will know about Floyd's secret, it will be Morgan."

Jaxson smiled. "Tomorrow it is. Maybe you can call Trevor and ask if he can meet us in Witch's Cove."

"I will, though I'm not sure how long Trevor said he'd be in Liberty."

Jaxson smiled. "You won't know until you call him."

"Fine. I'll ask if he can meet us tomorrow at say, noon?"

"Works for me," Jaxson said.

I pulled in front of the store and let him out. "Thanks for coming with me."

"I enjoyed it." Jaxson headed back inside. I really appreciated that Drake was willing to let his brother come on my adventure, especially when the shop was bound to be busy.

Because Aunt Fern had probably crawled into bed to watch some of her television shows, I didn't want to disturb her, but when I entered my apartment, who should be feeding Iggy and Aimee but my aunt. "This is a surprise," I said.

"Oh, I hope you don't mind, dear. Harold was trying to sleep and Aimee here was a bit chatty."

Okay. Maybe my aunt was losing it. Even if Iggy and I could see Uncle Harold, that didn't mean I believed a ghost needed quiet time to sleep. Heck, I didn't even think ghosts slept at all.

"What did you learn?" Iggy asked.

I detailed everything I could—that was, all but my visit to Gertrude Poole. Iggy would be upset that I didn't believe he'd done a good job, when in reality he had. "I'm about to call Trevor Whitehall and ask if he'd be willing to join Jaxson and me tomorrow for a chat with Morgan. If he's around his twin, I'm hoping he'll be visible longer."

"What do you think Morgan can tell you?" Aunt Fern asked.

"I'm hoping I'll learn why Floyd Paxton needed spells put on two necklaces. I also want to know where those necklaces are."

"That sounds like a good idea," she said.

Iggy jumped down from his stool where he was eating some arugula leaves. "I'm coming with you. I can see ghosts. I'll be able to talk to him."

Iggy had a point. It might even take less energy for Morgan to talk to Iggy than to me. "Sounds good."

He performed two tight circles. "I can't wait."

We all laughed. Tomorrow would be a very interesting day.

Chapter Fifteen

"WHERE IS HE?" I asked, as I paced in front of my car.

"Calm down. He'll be here," Jaxson said.

"Trevor said he was coming from Pine Grove, and that he'd leave at nine this morning to make it in time. He should have been here thirty minutes ago."

Jaxson looked around. "I doubt Morgan is just sitting around waiting to appear."

I still didn't have a good grasp on what ghosts could or couldn't do. "I don't see Morgan, though I didn't call to him either. The first time we met he was just there." Iggy leapt from the front seat to the pavement. "Where are you going?" I asked.

"I might be able to sense him better than you humans."

"Sounds reasonable, but don't go too far. Once Trevor arrives, I'll need you to help me."

He lifted a toe to his face and then placed it back on the pavement. I'm guessing it was as close to a salute as he could give. Iggy trotted off. Knowing my familiar, he would try to talk to Morgan, but I had no idea if he could conjure up the ghost or not.

At quarter to one, I called Trevor again.

"Hey," he said. "I am so sorry. I was on my way to

Witch's Cove when I got an emergency call from a hospital. One of the machines I sold them broke, and they need it repaired immediately. Can we do this another time?"

I swallowed my disappointment. "Ah, sure. I don't think Morgan is going anywhere." I looked up at Jaxson. He tilted his head with partially closed eyes. I didn't like the look. "Call when you can reschedule."

"I will." He disconnected. I pocketed my phone and told Jaxson the news. "Maybe we should contact Morgan anyway."

"Or we could ask Emma if she'd be willing to be a ghost booster of sorts. She's a relative, and she seemed willing to help before."

"I hate to disturb her, but it might give her some closure if she could talk to him one more time—through me, of course. I doubt she had the chance to say a proper goodbye."

Jaxson placed a hand on my shoulder. "I totally agree. I mean, if you could once more talk to someone who'd passed, wouldn't you jump at the chance?"

My hand automatically clasped my pink diamond that I always wore around my neck, and tears welled in my eyes. "Yes. My grandmother."

"There you go. All Emma can say is no. Call her."

"I wish I knew what to say."

Jaxson peered down at me. "How about the truth? Anytime anyone is totally honest with me, I tend to give in."

I never would have guessed Jaxson was such a softy. "Okay, but let's sit in the car. It's hot in the sun." I pulled out my phone, found Emma's number and called her, though I wasn't sure she'd even answer.

It rang and rang. Finally, she picked up. "Glinda, is everything okay?"

"Yes and no." I explained about wanting to talk with Morgan. "He has a hard time staying in his human-like form. I've heard if someone related to him is close by, he can draw energy from that person. I asked his twin brother to meet us, but he had an emergency he had to attend to. I was wondering if maybe you could meet us in Witch's Cove."

"You've spoken with Andy?"

"Andy? Ah…his name is Trevor."

"I'm afraid you're mistaken. Whatever name he is using, don't trust him. He's trouble."

My heart raced at the speed of light. Needing some support, I immediately put the phone on speaker so Jaxson could hear. "What can you tell me about Morgan's twin?"

"He and Morgan don't speak, but I know Andy has been in and out of jail for the last ten years."

Whoa! "He told me he was a medical sales representative and that he was never told he had a twin brother."

Emma's laugh sounded like it came from my arch nemesis, the Wicked Witch of the West. "Andy lied. He's good at that. Have you met him?"

"Yes." I tried to remember the exact day we saw him on the courthouse steps, but this past week had been a blur. "He said he had no idea that he even had a twin until he saw Morgan's picture in the paper or on the TV, I can't remember which."

"You need to tell the police."

Jaxson leaned over. "Jaxson here. What would we tell them? Do you know if he's done anything illegal?"

"No, but I'm sure he has."

The problem was that we needed proof before Steve could do anything. Only then did I remember that when I was about to tell Morgan about his twin brother that the ghost disappeared. My mother had communicated with Morgan and had mentioned his twin, but I have no idea his response. "We really need you to help us keep Morgan visible. He might know what his brother is up to."

"I don't think he's seen Andy in a long time, but I'm willing to try. Where should we meet?"

Considering Morgan didn't know who'd shot him, he couldn't point a finger at his brother. Even if he could, his testimony wouldn't be admissible in court.

"How about the parking lot next to the Bubbling Cauldron Coffee Shop? You don't even need to get out of your car. At least I don't think you do."

"I'll leave right now."

"Thank you."

As soon as I hung, up, Iggy came prancing out, his head high. I knew that look. "Morgan and I had a nice chat," he bragged.

"What? I hope you didn't wear him out."

"I don't know if I did, but did you know he knows all about his brother? Morgan says his name is Andy, not Trevor."

"I just learned that fact too. What did he say about him?" I could tell this would take a while and require several bribes to get him to reveal everything."

Jaxson touched my shoulder. "What is Iggy saying?"

I forgot that since Jaxson wasn't a warlock, he couldn't hear the little scoundrel. I relayed Iggy's comments. "I'll try to repeat the information." I looked over at Iggy. "Tell me more."

"Morgan was being a bit tight-lipped, if ghosts even have lips. Before we talked about *Andy*, I asked about the spell on the necklaces, and he said that his uncle gave him one of the necklaces, because if he should ever need money, he could sell it to one of his clan members for a really high price."

I repeated what Iggy said. "Clan member? Did Morgan tell you whether his uncle was in a motorcycle gang or something?" I asked.

"He wasn't specific. All Morgan said was that Floyd met with them every month."

"Where?"

"In the Hendrian National Forest." He stood taller. "Where I used to live."

He didn't have to say when he used to be green. I turned to Jaxson. "Do you know anything about a gang meeting in the Hendrian National Forest every month? I didn't realize there were a lot of trails for motorcycles in there."

"I think motorcycle enthusiasts don't care about trails. Florida is flat, which works well for them," Jaxson said. "But no, I haven't heard about any gangs near there—even when I was in prison."

I looked back down at Iggy. "Anything else?"

"His brother is trouble. Morgan said that Andy visited his Uncle Floyd one time, reminding him that he was three minutes older than Morgan, and that if anyone was to inherit the farm, it should be him."

I swallowed hard. Once more I told Jaxson the information.

"Do you think Trevor, or rather Andy, killed Morgan?" Jaxson asked.

I answered, even though his question might have been addressed to Iggy. "It's possible. It might be why he decided not to come today. He feared his dead brother would out him."

Jaxson slapped his thigh. "If Andy killed Morgan over the farm—which we don't know is true—he might come after Emma next."

A band squeezed tight around my chest. "You're right. I should warn her."

"When she gets here, we'll tell her. I don't think Andy knows where she's been staying, or he would have killed her by now."

"I'm not sure he would have—at least I don't think he'd shoot her in the back. That would put the spotlight on him too much. He might have assumed he would be next in line since Emma had disappeared months before. We need to do something to help."

"I think you should tell Steve," Jaxson said.

"And tell him what?"

"That you found Emma, and you believe Morgan's twin might have killed him. Tell him that Andy might even be after Emma as we speak."

Even I knew that wouldn't go over well. If Steve didn't think I was a crackpot before, he'd think it after I told him that bit of news. However, if what we conjectured was true, and Trevor harmed Emma, I couldn't live with myself. "Okay." I slipped out of the front seat. "Wish me luck."

"Luck. I'll keep Emma safe should she arrive before you

get back."

I rushed off to the sheriff's department, hoping Iggy would be okay staying with Jaxson.

When I entered the office, I was surprised to see Pearl at her desk. I thought she took Sunday's off.

Steve's grandmother looked up. "Oh, my. What happened? You look like you've seen a ghost."

Normally, that would have been funny, but not today. "I wish. I think Emma Paxton might be in trouble."

"Emma is alive?"

My aunt was slipping if she didn't let the gossip queens know. "Yes, and she's on her way here as we speak. Is the sheriff around?"

"No, hon. He had a domestic dispute he needed to deal with."

"I have to call him."

If Andy found out about Emma coming here, he might show up, and I'd need Steve to interfere. Though shooting Emma in the middle of town would be the dumbest thing Morgan's twin could do. It was possible that if he somehow learned of our meeting, he'd hang out nearby to see if we contacted Morgan.

"I'll give Steve a shout for you," Pearl said.

I jerked back to the present. "Thanks. Tell him I have some information on Morgan's murder."

Before she had the chance to ask me what that was, I rushed back to the parking lot. Thank goodness Jaxson had come with me today. I could only hope that if Andy showed up there wouldn't be any violence. On the plus side, Jaxson had a lot more muscles than Morgan's brother despite both having served time.

"What did Steve say?" Jaxson asked.

"He wasn't there, but Pearl is calling him to let him know we need him."

"Good. So now what?" Jaxson asked.

"We need to wait for Emma and see what Morgan can tell us."

As if I'd conjured her, she arrived and immediately jumped out of the car. I guess, she didn't care if anyone saw her.

"Is Morgan here?" she asked looking around.

"I haven't called him yet." There was no need to say Iggy had already spoken with him. "I need to ask him a few questions before you converse with him. Okay?"

She nodded. "I understand."

"Good." I inhaled and faced Emma. "I'm going to call Morgan, but I'll pretend to be talking to you."

To her credit, she didn't bat an eye. "That way no one will know you're contacting a ghost, right?"

"Exactly." I called Morgan's name a few times. Five seconds later, he materialized right next to Emma. I grinned. "He's here."

Morgan looked over at me. "I can't believe Aunt Emma is here."

"She wanted to say her goodbyes." I wasn't sure that was true, but I bet it was. "I've heard that you can draw on her energy to help stay in your kind-of-human form longer."

"Really? Who knew?"

"I know, right? I'm not sure how you do it, though. You'll have to experiment a bit."

Emma looked over at me. "What did he say?"

"He's really excited to see you. Morgan is now wrapping an arm around your shoulders. Oh, my, I can see him better now."

Morgan smiled for the first time. He was a handsome man. It was such a shame someone killed him. "Are you feeling better?" I asked him.

"Yes, much."

Emma looked right and the left. "I felt a chill, but I can't see him."

"That means he's here. If you feel a little queasy, that's to be expected," I told her. Not wanting to waste his energy, I turned back to Morgan. "I'm afraid I found out I was duped by your twin brother."

He laughed, or rather what I thought sounded like a rueful laugh came from his open mouth. "Don't believe anything that scoundrel tells you. One time, he visited Uncle Floyd and pretended to be me. Trust me when I say it didn't turn out well. The worse part was that my uncle told Andy about these necklaces and just how special they were. Uncle Floyd never would have revealed that secret to Andy."

When he said nothing else, I needed to urge him on. I had no idea how long he'd be able to communicate. "Yikes."

"What did Morgan say?" Emma asked.

I kept forgetting that no one could hear Morgan but me and Iggy. When I mentioned the necklaces, her face turned beet red. "That little jerk."

I would have used stronger words. "I agree." I turned back to Morgan. "Do you know where the necklaces are now?"

"I do."

Chapter Sixteen

I HELD MY breath, waiting for Morgan to tell me where to find the necklaces. I figured if I could see one, I might be able to understand what it could do.

"I don't know what happened to the necklace around my uncle's neck, but he gave me the other one."

The problem was that whoever had shot him might have robbed his house for that necklace. I had to tell him. "There was a break-in at your house after your death. The necklace might have been stolen." I repeated to the others what he'd said.

He shook his head. "No one could have found it. It's hidden under the floorboards which is covered over by an area rug. I told no one of its location. You need to find it and try to sell it to Charles. I have a feeling he stole the one around my uncle's neck after the wolves got to him."

Charles? "But if your uncle stole the first one, why would he want the second one?"

"Because everyone in the clan will want it. Charles is the only one who can find these people and sell it to them."

That made no sense. If Charles was bad, why do him a favor? I doubted there was time to ask him about it though. I swallowed hard. "Okay. Where exactly is the one you had?"

"With your back to the television stand, face the kitchen. Walk three steps forward and then turn right. The necklace is under the third floorboard."

Which was under an area rug. I made sure to repeat the instructions since I didn't know if I could remember them. "Okay, but do you know why your Uncle Floyd wanted the spell put on the necklaces in the first place?"

"To keep him from changing."

"To keep him from changing what?" I asked.

Emma sucked in a breath. "Oh, my goodness." She stumbled backward, and Jackson grabbed a hold of her shoulders to steady her.

"What is it?" Jaxson asked.

"It's true," she said.

"What's true?" I asked.

She gasped. "The hints, the leaving every full moon. I think Floyd was a werewolf."

Now I was speechless. Before I could think of what else to say, Steve Rocker rushed up to us. "Are you okay?" he asked me.

"I think so." I must have looked dazed. When I was about to ask Morgan if that was true, he disappeared. Again. Somehow our sheriff seemed to have that effect on ghosts.

"Are you Emma Paxton?" he asked. He must have had a photo of her.

Floyd's wife nodded. "Yes."

"We need to talk," the sheriff said.

That was an understatement, though I doubt Steve would believe anything she said, especially if she told him about werewolves.

"Boy do we ever," I chimed in. Jaxson seemed to be the only one who was keeping his cool. "I want Jaxson to come too. He's been with me on this journey almost the whole time."

Steve's lips thinned, implying he didn't trust Jaxson. Too bad.

"Fine," he said.

I motioned for Iggy to join me. When he rushed over, I scooped him up and dropped him into my bag. I was about to remind him that he should keep quiet, until I realized even if he spoke, no one but me could hear him.

When we all marched into the station, Pearl's eyes widened. I expected she'd want to chat with Emma, but she just stared instead.

"Let's sit in the conference room," Steve said. "Pearl, can you get us some water?"

I didn't realize he called her by her first name, though I suppose calling her grandma might have been a bit too informal.

She pushed back her chair. "Sure thing."

Like follow the leader, we walked single file into the conference room. I sat between Jaxson and Emma, while Steve sat across from us. It felt like an inquisition.

"Miss Goodall, since I imagine you are responsible for much of what has gone on today, maybe you'd like to tell us what happened."

Sorting through all of the events since we last spoke would not be easy, but I was going to try. This time, I'd leave nothing out—other than the fact that I spoke with Gertrude a second time or how Iggy contacted Morgan before I did. "I think I told you about the garnet necklaces that Gertrude Poole had put a spell on for Floyd."

Steve had a stack of yellow pads on the table. He pulled one over and then fished a pen out of his top pocket. I waited while he scribbled something down. I would have suggested he bring a laptop in here, but it was his department.

"You did. Go on," he said.

Someone knocked on the door, and Pearl entered with a tray full of glasses. She set them down. "I added a few cookies in case any of you get hungry." She smiled, turned around, and left.

I was very thankful for both the water and the plate of sweets. For the next fifteen minutes I detailed my movements, leaving out very few details. I had to give him credit for not questioning anything I said—until I was finished, of course.

"Emma, you said you believed your husband was a werewolf? Why is that?"

How could Steve ask that with such a straight face?

"It's a feeling. I mean, I never believed those kinds of creatures even existed, but when Floyd would take a break only on the full moon, together with the secrecy and the mention of some clan, what was I to think? And then he asked a witch to put a spell on some garnet necklace because he didn't want to hurt people? It sounded impossible yet plausible at the same time."

"I agree," Steve said. "In fact, when I lived in Overton, there were stories about motorcycle gangs living in the Hendrian National Forest—and about men who wore wolf masks. Now I'm not so sure they were masks."

Seriously? "You're saying you believe in werewolves?"

Even I wasn't convinced.

"I'm not saying one way or the other. I'm trying to gather the facts. To be honest, I have a harder time believing that you can talk to a ghost. Did Morgan give any more ideas as to who killed him?"

"No, though my money is on his twin brother," I said.

"Why is that?" Steve asked.

"Process of elimination." I repeated what I told Emma about who would want Morgan dead.

"I'll need evidence."

Of course, he did. "Morgan told me where to find one of the two necklaces." I then explained where it was.

"Since that is in Liberty, I'll call Misty. She'll need to go with you."

My heart dropped to my stomach. "Yes, yes. Of course. I'll need a screwdriver to pry up the board though."

He nodded. "I'll be happy to lend you one." Steve turned to Jaxson. "Go with her. It might take a bit of muscle to pry up a board."

Jaxson's expression remained stoic. "I will."

I snapped my fingers. "I have an idea on how we can catch Trev—I mean Andy—assuming he killed Morgan."

All eyes turned to me. "Is that so? How?" Steve asked.

While my plan hadn't been well-thought out, it was a plan—one that I believed would work. I outlined it the best I could. "Of course, I can't guarantee if Andy will respond the way I hope he will."

Emma smiled. "That scum? He'll take the bait."

"I hope so."

Steve turned back to Emma. "Mrs. Paxton, I'd like you to

stay in Witch's Cove for a while. For the next few days, I want you to stay at my house. I have a spare bedroom just for this purpose. I don't trust your nephew—the one who is alive that is."

Her shoulders sagged. "Neither do I. And thank you for believing me."

"Of course."

I didn't need any more encouragement to leave. Steve's blank face had unnerved me. Since my car was parked right outside, we took that. No surprise, Jaxson asked to drive. It was probably because I was still a bit shaky. I handed him the keys before sliding into the passenger seat.

Iggy popped his head out of my bag. "Wow, that was a trip."

His comment made me smile. "Why is that?" At least I didn't have to pretend that I could communicate with Iggy when I was around Jaxson.

"I think Steve almost believed you."

"You might be right."

"What did Iggy say?" Jaxson asked.

I told him. "I have to say, I thought I'd be met with a lot more resistance from our sheriff."

"If that necklace is where our ghost says it is, it will go a long way to establishing your credibility," Jaxson said.

"I agree." My stomach then grumbled. It was close to three, and I hadn't eaten since ten.

"How about we stop at a drive through? I could use a bite," he asked, though I suspected he suggested it because I sounded hungry.

Since that would be fast, I was good with it. "Fine, but we

can't dawdle. I don't want to keep the sheriff waiting."

The drive-thru was blessedly quick. When we arrived at Morgan's old house, I half expected our ghost to be sitting on the steps waiting for us. I had to remember to ask Uncle Harold how much energy it took to travel twenty miles.

Sheriff Misty Willows was parked in front of Morgan's house. "Let's do this," I said.

"Why do you sound so down? You should be excited," Jaxson said.

"More like nervous. What if the necklace isn't there? Does that mean I'm crazy, and that all of this ghost stuff is in my head?"

Jaxson chuckled. "No."

His answer came too quickly, but I let it be.

"I saw him too, remember," Iggy said, his head peeking out of the top of my bag.

"Thank you for reminding me, now stay down." I didn't need Misty to think of me as a loon, too.

"Hello," Misty Willows said as we walked up to her. "Steve said there's been a break in the case."

I didn't know if he'd said my information came from a ghost or not. In case he didn't, I decided to play it safe. "Yes. I'm hoping my source was correct in telling me where Morgan hid this valuable necklace."

"Let's check it out."

Misty sounded nice enough, just like she had the first time we met. I don't know why it bothered me a bit that she and Steve were working this case together, but it did. When we entered Morgan's house, the place was a mess. That was a shame. I had no idea who was responsible for cleaning it up, but I'm guessing it wouldn't be the Liberty sheriff's department.

Would the house now go to Emma? If I recall, he didn't have a will. Surely, Morgan wouldn't want his brother to have it or his uncle Charles for that matter.

Part of me wanted to take a photo to show Morgan, but there was no way I could explain that to Misty. "He said to start with my back to the television cabinet and walk forward…um." Darn. Why couldn't I remember how many steps? I never forgot a number.

"Three steps forward, turn right, and find the third floorboard," Jaxson said. "I'll lift the rug."

Thank goodness he was there. Since Morgan was taller than me, I took larger steps. One, two, three. Given the small living room, I don't think I could have taken four. I then turned to the right. As soon as Jaxson lifted up the rug, I didn't need to count anymore. One slat had small indents in the side. By the time I moved toward Jaxson, he was already prying up the board. It creaked and cracked.

"Careful," I said, though at this point in Morgan's life, I'm not sure if he cared.

"Got it." The board popped open, and I dropped to my knees to look into the space. "Holy moly."

Jaxson dug his hand down there and pulled out a plastic bag that contained the most gorgeous bejeweled necklace I'd ever seen. I couldn't believe that Floyd Paxton would wear this for even a minute. If I had to guess, he didn't want to, but if I believed all of the folklore surrounding werewolves, it meant he would be able to control his shift on the full moon. That alone might be worth it to him.

Misty slid the bag out of Jaxson's grasp. "Give me a second to photograph this, but don't worry, Steve told me that it was important that he keep it for a while. I believe you two have a sting operation to attend to."

"We do," I said.

I was more excited to bring down Andrew Oliver, aka Trevor Whitehall, than anything. To shoot one's brother in the back was downright cowardly—assuming he was guilty. I still couldn't figure out what he'd get out of it. Some money for a necklace? I was no expert in jewels, but the pretty garnet stones did not even look real. Or was he jealous that Morgan seemed to have a more charmed life? Or it could all come down to owning a hundred acres.

Chapter Seventeen

AFTER JAXSON AND I returned from Liberty and delivered the necklace to Steve, we went over the plan to catch Andy once more.

"I got this, Glinda," Steve said. "Don't worry. I've taken all of the precautions to make sure Emma is safe. If Andy is our man, we'll soon have enough evidence to convict him."

I did appreciate his self-confidence. "Thanks."

Emma nodded. "I know what to do, too. Tomorrow at three thirty, I will go to the Bubbling Cauldron and sit by the front window." She chuckled. "At least I know what Andy looks like. Should I feel threatened in any way, I'll signal Misty or her deputy to help."

Because Steve didn't have any backup, he'd asked if Misty and her deputy could assist. They would subdue Andy should he try anything.

"That all sounds good," I said.

Jaxson slipped a hand on my lower back. "Come on, Glinda. It's been a long day."

Darn. Just because I was full of questions and energy didn't mean Jaxson was. "Sure."

Jaxson escorted me across the street to the Tiki Hut Grill and said goodbye.

Once inside, I trudged up the stairs. At the top of the landing, I opened my purse. "Are you hungry?" I asked Iggy.

"What do you think?" Iggy sounded cranky, and I couldn't blame him. "Let's see if Aunt Fern wants to chat. I bet she might be able to scrounge up an extra hibiscus flower or two for you."

His little face perked up. "Great. Then I can tell Aimee everything."

For once I didn't mind him blabbing. It wasn't like Aimee could talk to many people anyway.

I knocked on my aunt's door, and she answered quickly. "Oh, good. You're back. You've been gone a long time."

"Yes, and we have a lot to tell you, but first, do you have any hibiscus flowers for Iggy? He's starving."

"I sure do."

Iggy jumped out of my purse and followed my aunt to the kitchen. From the bedroom, Aimee ambled out. "I thought I heard talking. Where have you both been today?"

While I appreciated that she could talk, I didn't need another busy body on this floor. "Once my aunt feeds Iggy, I'll tell all of you everything."

An hour later after a gazillion questions and hopefully with some good answers, I think my aunt and Aimee were caught up to speed. "Now, I'm going to take a hot bath and crash," I said.

"You should. If you want to take Monday off, you can.

"I appreciate the offer, but nothing is going to happen until after three."

She hugged me. "Suit yourself."

Iggy and I returned to my apartment. Once inside, I

headed to the bathroom to take that soak and to call Penny. I owed her a very long explanation about what had been happening. Once I told her, I asked her to keep a lid on this information for another few days. Thankfully, she promised she would.

AT ABOUT THREE thirty on Monday, Jaxson and I were sitting in a window booth at the Moon Bay Tea Shop keeping an eye on the coffee shop across the street. I could see Emma sitting close to the front window. What was my plan to catch Andy? Emma had agreed to use herself as bait. She was wearing Floyd's lovely red garnet necklace. Even though no one had prepped Miriam about our plan, I had no doubt that she would spread the word that not only was Emma Paxton alive, she was wearing a gorgeous necklace. Knowing Miriam, she'd conclude the necklace was a gift from an admirer, and it would kill her to not know who Emma was dating.

I just hoped that Emma could pull this off. It was hard to go undercover without looking overly nervous. Jaxson reached across the booth and placed his hand on mine. "Stop worrying. It's not like Andy will walk into the coffee shop and shoot her."

I returned my gaze to him, wondering if he could read minds now. "You're right. Then he'd go to jail and get nothing. Besides, Misty and another deputy will make sure Emma remains safe."

"Right. Now, enjoy your tea. Didn't Maude say it was your favorite brand?"

"She did."

After an hour, Emma stood, paid and then slowly walked to her car. She slid in and took off to Steve's house. Another Liberty deputy had been assigned to watch the house from across the street should Andy approach. I was sure that Steve was seriously wishing the town council would hurry up and hire help.

"Time to go, Glinda," Jaxson said.

I must have been spacing out. "I know, and thanks for doing this with me."

"You know me." He smiled.

I finished his thought. "Yes, it's better than ordering wine."

We both chuckled and left.

After I returned home and filled Iggy in on what was happening, he hopped up on his stool and faced me. "There has to be something we can do."

I didn't like that tone. "We've provided all of the ammunition for Steve to finish this—assuming Andy is guilty. I'm not some sworn officer of the law, so my hands are tied.

"Fine."

I knew what that meant. Iggy wanted to meddle. I might have objected, but at this stage I was desperate for a conclusion too. Morgan deserved to pass over and have a nice life, wherever that may be.

As tempted as I was to sit with the Liberty deputy and watch for Andy, I feared I'd only be in the way.

My cell rang a short while later. When I checked the caller ID, I smiled. It was Jaxson. I couldn't imagine what he wanted since we just left the tea shop. "Hey, there."

"Hey. It really bugged me that I wasn't able to dig up any dirt on Trevor Whitehall before."

"That's probably because the real Trevor Whitehall is a normal guy," I replied.

"He is at that. Andy must have found one of his business cards and stolen the man's name, which was why my check was superficial at best."

Did he want my forgiveness? "That's okay. It's not like it's your job to find information on people."

He chuckled. "I know, but it's called pride. Anyway, I did some deep diving on our real suspect, Andy Oliver."

He had my interest. "Do tell."

"He has quite the rap sheet—mostly B&E. He was accused of assault twice but was never convicted."

Either he was smart or just plain lucky. "Did you find any evidence that points to the fact he knows how to handle a weapon?"

"Give the girl a gold star. I did. In fact, I found a photo of him winning a ribbon at a shooting range competition."

"Well, I'll be. That means he could have shot his brother." Note, I wasn't saying he did for sure, just that he had a good chance of hitting his target. "Why don't you text Steve what you found. It might make him act with more caution," I said.

"Why me?"

I had an answer for that. "If you plan to live in this community, it's good to have law enforcement think favorably of you."

He didn't answer for a second. "I like the way you think. I'll send Steve the information now."

"Great. And thanks again for all your help."

"Always." Jaxson disconnected.

Because I'd not had dinner yet, I thought I'd head to the Spellbound Diner. It never hurt to help spread the word about Emma and her newly acquired necklace.

I WAITED TWO days! Two very long days and still no move on Andy Oliver's part. Maybe I had been wrong about him wanting to harm Emma. If only I understood his end game, I might be able to figure out his next move. By killing his own brother, he had either wanted the necklace, or he had wanted the property. With Emma dead, he'd get both.

It was bad enough that Morgan's killer hadn't been brought to justice. Now I probably looked like some whacko to Steve.

When someone knocked on my door, both Iggy and I jerked. It wasn't Aunt Fern's knock. Hers was delicate. Besides, she would open the door and come in. This sounded like it belonged to a man. "Who is it?"

I really needed better security. What if it was Andy?

"It's Steve."

The relief weakened my knees. I quickly scanned my tiny space. It didn't look as if I'd just cleaned, but it wasn't a mess either. I shouldn't care what he thought of where I lived, but I did. "Coming."

I rushed to the door and pulled it open. Iggy hopped off his stool but remained at a respectable distance. He'd been hit by the door one too many times.

"Sheriff, come in." I did a quick scan of his face, hoping to learn the reason for the visit. He looked happy. That was a relief.

"I have news. I realize it will be all over town by morning, but I want you to be the first to hear it."

My heart pounded. "Sit down, please. Can I get you something to drink? Water, tea, a beer? Or maybe some wine?"

Being this nervous wasn't really like me, but this was Steve Rocker. Big Steve Rocker. In my house.

He chuckled. "Water would be great."

I wanted something stronger, but that wouldn't be polite. I carried the drinks in, handed him the glass, and then sat on the single chair next to the sofa. "What's your news?"

I could only hope that meant something good had happened.

"We caught Andy in the act." He grinned.

I was so dumbfounded that I couldn't even speak for a few seconds. "Really, how?"

"I heard from Nate Billows that Andy Oliver had checked into the Magic Wand Hotel, which put me on high alert."

"Did you give Nate or Ted a photo of Andy?"

"I did. I figured if Andy planned to do any harm to Emma, he needed to be close to town."

I smiled. "I have to hand it to you."

He tapped the side of his head. "That's part of my charm. People underestimate me."

I doubted that, but I kept my mouth shut. "How did you catch Andy?"

"If you recall, I had asked Emma to stay with me."

"I do."

"I asked her to leak that information to Miriam. The gossip queens then went to town. The truth was that Emma was bunking with Pearl, who for once was able to keep that a secret."

I laughed. "Probably the hardest job she's ever had."

His cheeks dimpled when he smiled. "Probably also true. Anyway, I got the call from Misty's deputy that Andy was on his way to my house, though I doubt he had any idea I lived there."

"Probably not, though I'm surprised he didn't check." I waved a hand. "It doesn't matter. Go on."

"As I had suspected, he climbed in the back window that I'd conveniently left unlatched. I also had put several pillows under the blanket to make it look like Emma was asleep, and I even had Pearl lend me an old wig of hers."

I had to hand it to him. He'd altered my plan and made it better. "That is brilliant. Then what?"

"Then Andy took aim and shot the pillows three times. I plan to ask the town to reimburse me for my thin comforter and my three old pillows."

I laughed. "Did you rush in and arrest him?"

"After the deputy stepped out of the closet and cuffed him, I did."

I clapped. "I love it."

"I sent his gun to the lab to check to see if the bullet that killed my pillows are the same as those that killed Morgan."

At the mention of his name, I sobered. "Did Andy say why he wanted Emma dead?"

"It was what you said. He thought he should be the next

one in line for the property. This intended killing was to make it look like a robbery—only we stopped him before he could trash the bedroom and the house. Andy said he wanted the necklace so he could sell it. I'm guessing he believed that with Emma dead, he'd show surprise and shock when he was given the property."

"That is sick. Didn't he think Charles would object? I imagine Floyd's own brother would have more right to the land than anyone."

"I don't know." Steve polished off his glass of water and stood. "I wanted to let you know that you did a good job with this, but it would be a lot safer if you stuck to waitressing."

"I agree. Just so you know, I didn't ask to be able to see ghosts. It was actually a bit disconcerting. And I certainly never thought a dead person would ask me for my help in solving a crime."

"Good to know. I'll let you get back to whatever you were doing. Goodnight."

I thought about asking him to stay a bit, but he probably had a ton of paperwork to fill out. "Oh, Steve?"

He spun around. "Yes."

"What's going to happen to the necklace?"

"I imagine the courts will see fit to let Emma keep it."

That was what I was afraid of. "I'm not sure that's such a good idea."

"What do you mean?"

"Everyone in town knows she has it. We don't need one of those werewolves trying to get it from her."

His brows rose. "Oh, yeah. The werewolves. Do you think they exist?"

"I don't know, but it's better to be safe than sorry," I said.

"Good point."

"According to Gertrude and Morgan, there were two necklaces. Do we know who has the second one?" I asked. "Since Floyd was killed on a full moon, maybe he was wearing it to prevent him from shifting into a werewolf. If his killer took it, it should be somewhere, right?" I was still struggling with the concept of shapeshifters.

He quickly sobered. "That makes sense. Find the necklace. Find his killer—assuming it was a human who turned into an animal."

The look of dismay on Steve's face almost hurt me in its intensity. "If someone was willing to kill for Floyd's necklace, Emma is still in danger."

"I'll suggest to Emma that I put the necklace in a safety deposit box at the bank. She won't have access of it, at least until we can figure out this werewolf thing."

I nodded. "That would be for the best."

He stepped toward me, and my heart flipped. "Glinda, I want to say I'm sorry I doubted you."

I never expected to hear that from him. Ever. "That's okay. You've been amazingly open-minded. I'm not sure I'd be the same if I didn't see or hear things the way I do."

"So, we're good?"

What did that mean? "Absolutely."

"Let's hope the next time you stop in to chat, it won't be to report a murder, say you've had another ghost sighting, or heaven forbid you claim to have seen a man change into a werewolf."

He did have a vivid imagination. "I hope so too."

Chapter Eighteen

One week later

I WAS SITTING in the Bubbling Cauldon Coffee shop after I finished my shift when who should walk in but Sheriff Steve Rocker. I will admit that a trickle of excitement charged through me. He was a handsome man, but not one I wanted to be with. Why? His life was full of danger, and I'm not sure I could handle that on a daily basis.

I half expected him to smile and walk on by, but once inside, he strode right over to my table. "May I join you?"

It wasn't like I was about to turn him down. "Of course."

"Have you spoken with Morgan again?" he asked.

When he didn't grin or wink, he must have been serious. "Once. I told him that his brother had killed him, and I gave him my best guess as to why."

"What did he say?" Steve asked with complete sincerity.

"He figured as much. While he'd wished it had been some random violent act, he thanked me for helping."

"Is he now able to cross over as they say?" he asked.

I was in a bit of shock at this new Steve Rocker. "I can't say for sure. I've tried a few times to contact him, but he hasn't appeared, so maybe he has. I know that Morgan wanted closure, and now he has it."

Steve nodded. "I see."

That sounded like something else had happened. "Why?"

"I'm glad Morgan knows. Turns out Andy Oliver is not a fan of spending the rest of his life behind bars. He was willing to bargain with us—or rather with the county courts—for the ability to be paroled at some point."

That caught my interest as I sipped on my ice coffee. "What did he have to bargain with?"

"Knowledge. He said he was at Floyd's house when Charles showed up the day Floyd was murdered. Floyd had gone outside to meet with his brother because Andy was in the house. That was when he heard his uncles argue about the necklace. Floyd was wearing his, but he wouldn't say where the other one was. Ever curious, Andy peeked out the window and watched as Charles transformed into a werewolf. A second later, Floyd turned, too."

I leaned forward, my heart pounding. "Does that mean we should believe werewolves are real?" I whispered.

"Maybe. I know Emma thinks they are. You said Morgan claimed his uncle needed a spell put on the necklaces because he didn't want to change. I don't know how else to explain it. I'd like to say it's all hogwash, but what if it isn't?"

I sucked in a breath, the clues coming together. "That's why Floyd had blood under his fingernails. I bet the blood will match Charles' blood."

"I thought the same thing. That's why I asked a few lawmen from the county to round up Charles and test his blood. And guess what? It matched what was found under Floyd's fingernails."

"I'll be." I ran that scenario through my head. "Do you

think the courts will believe werewolves exist?"

"Probably not. I'm guessing Charles would say he and his brother got into an altercation in which Floyd scratched Charles."

I could fill in the blanks. "And Charles would say he left after the fight. Afterward, the wolf attacked and killed his brother."

Steve pointed a finger at me. "That is why I suggested they search Charles' house for the other necklace." He smiled.

"Don't tell me they found it."

"They did. I'm not sure we can make the murder charge stick, but I'm hoping the theft of the necklace will hold."

I shook my head. "I'm not sure people will believe that farmer Floyd would wear such a necklace. Charles probably will say he inherited it, maybe from their mother or grandmother."

"We'll see. At least we know the truth. It's possible that Emma can testify that Floyd bought the necklaces, and that they weren't family heirlooms."

"Unless they were."

"There is that. All we can do it try," he said.

"I agree, and thanks for telling me. I love it when loose ends are tied up."

He tapped the table and stood. "Thanks to you, they are. We need to catch up some time."

I wasn't positive what that meant, but I liked the sound of it. "For sure."

No sooner had Steve left than Emma Paxton waltzed in. I had to admit, a bit of rest had done wonders for her. Her hair was styled, and she was wearing what looked like a new dress.

I waved. "Emma!" I motioned her to join me.

She smiled. "I thought I saw you in the window." As she pulled out a chair to sit, she waved to the server. "I have news."

I wanted to tell her about Andy's information and about Charles' arrest, but I'd let Steve do the honors. Emma seemed ready to burst. "Do tell."

While I wasn't a gossip queen like some others who shall remain nameless, I loved to hear things.

The server came over and took Emma's order. "You'll never guess who stopped by the farmhouse."

I had no idea. "Who?"

"Joe Delaney."

I didn't even know how to react. "Is that a good thing or a bad thing? Did I hear correctly that you decided not to sell the farm?"

"That's true. Turns out my miserly husband had been saving his money—a lot of it—that he'd never told me about. I can now afford to hire some ranch hands to take care of the place."

"I couldn't be happier for you."

"It gets even better. Once Joe learned that I wasn't going to budge about selling, he finally told me the real reason why he was so anxious to buy my land."

Steve might have thought all of the loose ends had been tied up, but he was wrong. The whole issue with Joe's apparent desire for Floyd's land still bothered me. Now, I'd find out the truth. "Tell me."

"He found one of his grandfather's old journals that he'd only glanced through in the past. I can't remember what he said prompted him to look, but when he read it, he learned that two of his relatives were rather notorious."

My pulse soared. I couldn't believe it. "Don't tell me it was Mary and James Delaney, the famous bank robbers?"

Her mouth dropped open. "You know about them?"

I gave her a brief rundown of what I had learned. "At one time I thought maybe Joe had killed Morgan so he could search the land without interference."

She waved a hand. "Nonsense. He is the nicest man. Why I never figured it out when I was married to Floyd, I don't know."

Emma's blush told it all. She liked him. "What did Joe want?"

"He has a map that shows where those two bank robbers buried their take on my property. If I let him search, he'll split it with me."

"That's fantastic." I didn't want to bring up the fact that the amount of money from the early 1900s might not be as great as they would hope. Also, I had no idea about any statute of limitations on money found from a bank robbery. Far be it for me to burst her happy bubble.

When the server delivered Emma's drink, she held it up in a toast. I lifted my cup and tapped hers. "To the best amateur sleuth in all of Witch's Cove," she said.

I laughed. "I might be the only one, but I will take the title anyway. And thank you for your help in solving this crime. We couldn't have done it without you."

"You're welcome. May the rest of the year be devoid of any more murders."

I'd toast to that, though I had a sneaking suspicion that

wouldn't be the case. We chatted a bit more about what her plans were for the future. While I thoroughly enjoyed talking with her, I couldn't wait to tell Jaxson what I had learned. When he had become important in my life, I don't know. I had to say, I was looking forward to the future.

I hope you enjoyed meeting the townsfolk of Witch's Cove, and Glinda's cute familiar, Iggy, but don't worry, she will be running into trouble soon.

Glinda promises to keep out of trouble, but when the powerful witch, Gertrude Poole, asks for Glinda's help, she can't resist finding what the pink aura means.

Check out The Mystery of the Pink Aura (book 3 of A Witch's Cove Mystery.)

Don't forget to sign up for my Cozy Mystery newsletter *to learn about my discounts and upcoming releases. If you prefer to only receive notices regarding my releases, follow me on BookBub.*
http://smarturl.it/VellaDayNL
bookbub.com/authors/vella-day

Here is a chapter one of The Mystery of the Pink Aura.

PENNY CARSTED, MY coworker and best friend, rushed up to me and tugged on my sleeve, clearly needing my attention. "Glinda, did you hear?"

I set the full sugar shaker down on the side table in the Tiki Hut Grill where we both waitressed and faced her. Despite her out loud squeal, my heart didn't race because I knew everything was a big deal to Penny. It was one of the many reasons why I adored her. "Hear what?"

"We have a new deputy!"

Okay, I hadn't expected that announcement, and I will admit my pulse actually jumped. "It's about time. What do we know about him?" I asked, letting my never-ending curiosity get the best of me.

I assumed the new addition to the sheriff's department was male, because the Witch's Cove city council was responsible for hiring this person. And, well, let's say our beloved rulers were basically a good old boys club.

Why did I care? I had recently *unofficially* worked with Sheriff Steve Rocker on a case that involved the murdered nephew of one of our very own, and I wanted to make sure the city council hired someone who would be an asset. At least, that was what I told myself.

Why did I assume Penny would know about this new

arrival? Easy. Even on the day of the deputy's arrival, the whole town would have learned if he was married—did or did not have kids—what his favorite foods were, and what his shirt size was. The last statistic might seem strange to the average person, but the five gossip queens of Witch's Cove were all single, and it wouldn't be unkind of me to say that four of the five had a roaming eye. It wasn't just me who thought that. All of them would readily admit it too, especially Dolly Andrews, the owner of the Spellbound Grill.

My sixty-three-year-old Aunt Fern was the exception. She claimed she wasn't looking for a man, but I think if the right person came along, she might change her mind. While I now had the ability to see her husband's ghost, I think Uncle Harold would want her to be happy too.

"What do I know?" Penny asked, finally answering me. "Nothing, nada, zilch, and that is the problem. What is happening to this town?"

I chuckled to cover up my embarrassment that I hadn't heard even that much. "You have no information other than he's arrived?"

"No, and to make matters worse, I ran into Dolly, and she only knew that he came into town late last night. Apparently, there are no stats on him—including what his name is."

Wow. That was a first. Clearly, these women were slacking. "Let's ask Aunt Fern," I suggested. A person couldn't sneeze in town without everyone learning about it in part because my nosy aunt had a direct line to the sheriff's grandmother, Pearl Dillsmith, who happened to be the receptionist at the sheriff's department. I figured that intel was as good as anyone could get. Pearl would have met this newcomer and hopefully would have told her friends all about him already.

If the information flow was ever slow in coming from her gossipy friends, my aunt, who owned the Tiki Hut Grill, would hear about it from someone in her restaurant.

At the moment, she was working the checkout counter. Since she wasn't helping anyone, both Penny and I went up to her.

"Hey, Aunt Fern." Needing to make a bit of small talk first to grease the wheel so to speak, I peeked over the counter to see if her newly adopted cat, Aimee, was keeping her company. She was not, and that concerned me a bit. "Is Aimee with Iggy?"

Iggy was my familiar—a very chatty pink iguana—who considered himself a sleuth. As ridiculous as that might sound, he did have a knack for finding useful information.

"I doubt it. I think they had another fight."

"I hadn't heard about it." Why was I being left out of everything? My heart ached for my poor familiar. Iggy really liked Aimee. Even though this new arrival had only recently been given the magical power of speech, she was still a cat—one who gave affection only when she saw fit. "What can you tell me about the new deputy?" I asked.

My aunt's eyes suddenly brightened. It was because she loved being the disseminator of gossip. "According to Pearl, he is quite the looker. Dark haired, olive skinned, and he has the bluest eyes she's even seen."

Considering Pearl was in her late seventies, I'm not so sure I could trust her description. "Apart from his dashing good looks, what do we know about him?"

"He's from Montana."

That was a far cry from Florida. "Then I don't blame him for wanting a change of scenery." That wasn't quite the information I was looking for, but it was better than nothing.

"What else, Fern?" Penny asked. "Does this handsome stranger have a name?"

A blank look crossed her face. "You know, I don't think Pearl mentioned it. I think the sheriff came in when she was giving me the deets, but don't you worry, I'll find out what I can and let you two know."

Penny smiled. "Thanks."

I motioned to Penny that we get out of the way of the customer who had just walked up with his bill and credit card in hand.

"Did you teach her to say *deets*?" I whispered as I guided us back to the condiment table.

"Yes. If she's ever going to attract a man, she needs to sound hip."

I barked out a short laugh. "My aunt isn't looking to date."

Penny waved a hand. "Everyone is looking."

There was no use arguing with her. We had been friends for three years, and once Penny made up her mind, there was no changing it. I might have pressed the issue, but I had the feeling my aunt enjoyed the hip-speak lessons.

Just as I was about to speculate about this new Montana cowboy, the front doors flew open, and I swear a whole busload of people rushed in. My aunt thanked the customer at the counter and then hustled over to the newcomers to find tables for all of them. She didn't need to tell us it was time to move into action. We knew the drill.

As I spun around to get back to work, my pink tiara shifted on my head and nearly fell off. Why was I wearing cheap plastic headgear? Simple. All employees were required to wear a costume. Aunt Fern had believed it would help draw in the tourists, and she had been right. Without a doubt, business had picked up ever since we had started dressing up for work.

Why a pink tiara, you might ask? My mother was a *Wizard of Oz* fanatic, which was why she named me Glinda. It made sense too since I am a witch—albeit not a great one—and we live in the south. Even though I was teased a lot growing up for having that name, I eventually grew to like it, mostly because the movie witch always wore pink—my favorite color.

"Glinda!" my aunt called. "Table one, four, and seven are waiting."

Daydreaming was my worst flaw—or rather one of my worst. "On my way."

I loved being a waitress, but only when I had the time to chat with the customers. Today, however, would not give me that rush since there wouldn't be time to make any sort of connection. I strode over to table one. I'd never seen this couple before, so I suspected they were tourists.

"Hey there. I'm Glinda. Are you here for our sandy beaches and brilliant sunshine?" I asked with practiced perfection.

"Not this time. We might take a dip in the Gulf, but we came for the dog show."

How could I have forgotten about that big event? It was

the first annual agility dog training competition in Witch's Cove. "Are you showing a dog?"

She chuckled. "Oh, no. We have a mutt who rarely follows directions, unless it's time to eat or go for a walk. But we love him to death." The woman, who was in her mid-forties, had bright purple hair streaked with pretty blue and green highlights. "I wish we could afford one of those agility dogs, but those pooches are too expensive for our blood."

"I hear ya." About not being able to afford a show dog, that is. I could never have a dog. Iggy would tease the poor pup to death. Not only that, my familiar wasn't big on competing for my affection. "I look forward to checking out the show after work. It should be fun. What can I get you?" I couldn't afford to dawdle today.

After they ordered, I headed over to my next table. This was a family of four who were also here for the dog show, but these were competitors. "Our dog won in Delmar, so he's ready to compete in this Masters Class competition," the mother said.

"That's amazing." Though I had no idea our show was at that level. "What kind of dog is he?"

"Snookums is a Papillon."

Snookums? I shouldn't be one to judge. Maybe it was why I gave Iggy a boring name—or so he reminded me all of the time. I didn't want to admit I'd never heard of that breed. "I wish you luck."

"Thanks."

I really needed to find out more about this event. I'd been so busy trying to solve the mystery of who killed Morgan Oliver last month, that I hadn't kept up on current events. I had heard that Eleanor Aldrich was in charge of this dog event, and that it was supposed to bring in a lot of revenue to the town. I just never took the time to find out the details. I'd have to ask Iggy tonight what he knew. Between him and his no-longer girlfriend—the talking cat—they might know.

"What can I get you?" I asked.

After pouring over the menu, they finally ordered. Before I took the order at my third table, I dropped the first two requests off at the kitchen. While I was happy for Aunt Fern and her bottom line, having only Penny with me to handle all ten inside tables was hectic at best. I was sure the two outside patio servers had it just as bad though.

As I approached table seven, I glanced over at Penny who seemed more stressed than I was. She was already a bit high-strung, probably because she had to raise a seven-year-old mostly by herself. Her ex-husband helped with taking and picking up Tommy at school, but not much else.

The forty-five to fifty-year-old gentleman at my table was wearing a pair of navy-blue slacks and a well-pressed white shirt with gold cuff-links. I couldn't remember the last time I'd seen this kind of attire during the hot summer months—especially in here. His nails were polished and his eyebrows manscaped. Most people probably didn't notice those kind of details, but wild hair randomly jutting above a person's eyes disturbed me.

Since the man had placed the many-paged menu on the table and looked up, I figured he was ready.

"Hi there, I'm Glinda, what can I get you?" He didn't look like the type who desired a conversation.

"A coffee with a quarter teaspoon of cinnamon and a

dollop of cream—but don't overdo it. And some real sugar, please. I don't use that *fake* stuff." He tugged on his long sleeves, probably to show off that he had money. "I'll have the baked fish. Please ask the chef not to dry it out."

He was a piece of work, but I'd met worse. "Sure thing. Are you here for the dog show?" I'd learn that this influx of folks all seemed to have come for that.

"Yes. My Mittens is one of the contestants. He's a Border Collie. Keep an eye on him. He's a winner." I couldn't decide if he actually smiled, or if he had gas.

"I can't wait." Or not.

There was something off-putting about this man, but why should it matter? I'd promised myself that I was finished with sticking my nose in where it didn't belong.

As I scurried to the kitchen to drop off his order, my aunt motioned me over. "Yes?"

"Table six needs more coffee and table nine says the food is cold," my aunt said, sounding as stressed as I felt.

"I'll take care of it." I waved the orders to show her I wasn't slacking.

I started working here three years ago, right after I decided that being a middle school math teacher wasn't for me. All during that time, I don't remember it ever being this packed, especially in the middle of July when it rained pretty much every day.

Someone should have warned us that this many people would descend for this dog show. Who knew they were so popular?

For the next hour and a half until my shift ended, it was non-stop work. Not that I didn't appreciate the tips, but I couldn't chat with anyone since I was either taking orders or running food to the tables.

By the time the next set of servers showed up, I was tired, but not too tired to check out the new deputy.

It wasn't so much that I liked to snoop—or had an inner drive to snoop—but it was that I cared about our sheriff and wanted to make sure he was getting the help he deserved. Steve Rocker had only arrived in town seven weeks ago, but I'd quickly figured out he was one of the good guys. With the addition of this new deputy, Witch's Cove now had two newcomers.

I smiled. Steve Rocker had come a long way since his arrival. At first, he'd been skeptical about my ability to determine the cause of death by waving a pink crystal over the deceased's body, but eventually he stopped thinking of me as some crazy lady who considered herself a witch. Now, I think he sees me as a necessary evil.

After refilling the salt and pepper shakers once more, I clocked out. Since I lived on top of the restaurant in one of the two apartments, I ran upstairs to my place. Iggy, my familiar, was on his usual rattan stool looking out at the beach and the slightly overcast sky.

"A lot of people here for the dog show?" he asked without turning around. "It sounded loud downstairs."

I lifted off my tiara. "You have no idea." I explained about the dog show. "From what I gathered, it's two days of agility training and then the show itself. Good thing I have tomorrow off so I can check it out." Penny asked if I'd work Sunday for her. In exchange she'd work tomorrow for me. It was a win-win solution. "I'm too old to be working three days straight in this madhouse."

Twenty-six might seem young to most, but after learning I could suddenly see ghosts, I hadn't slept well. I needed a break.

After entering my bedroom, I changed out of my witch costume. I then pulled on a pair of dark pink shorts, a sleeveless rose top, and my pink sandals. If I didn't make it clear before, I like pink. In fact, I only wear pink.

After checking my wardrobe choice in the mirror to make sure I looked presentable, I returned to the living room. And no, I wasn't thinking about impressing our hot newcomer by putting on one of my better outfits.

Iggy turned around and hopped down from his stool. "Don't we look pretty."

I doubted it was a compliment. "I just changed into shorts."

"Uh-huh. I bet you're going to check out the new deputy, aren't you?" he asked in a teasingly sing-song voice.

How did everyone know about him but me? "What do you know?"

"Do you have any arugula leaves? I'm hungry."

Answer avoidance was a sure sign he was trying to exchange information for food. "I have to bribe you for information now? I thought we were partners."

Iggy had the decency to look away. A few seconds later, he looked back at me—or rather his eyes that were located on the side of his head faced me. I knew how to out stare him though.

"I would tell you more, but I don't know much. I'm waiting to see what everyone else learns," he said.

"Fine. I'll fix you some leaves, but next time, please be honest with me."

After I set out something for him to eat, I grabbed my keys and phone, ready to head out on my fact-finding mission. Once downstairs, I asked Aunt Fern for a ten-dollar gift certificate. I thought it would be fun to be the welcoming committee of one.

Buy THE MYSTERY OF THE PINK AURA

THE END

A WITCH'S COVE MYSTERY (Paranormal Cozy Mystery)

PINK Is The New Black (book 1)

A PINK Potion Gone Wrong (book 2)

The Mystery of the PINK Aura (book 3)

Sleuthing In The PINK (book 4)

HIDDEN REALMS OF SILVER LAKE (Paranormal Romance)

Awakened By Flames (book 1)

Seduced By Flames (book 2)

Kissed By Flames (book 3)

Destiny In Flames (book 4)

Box Set (books 1-4)

Passionate Flames (book 5)

Ignited By Flames (book 6)

Touched By Flames (book 7)

Box Set (books 5-7)

Bound By Flames (book 8)

Fueled By Flames (book 9)

Scorched By Flames (book 10)

FOUR SISTERS OF FATE: HIDDEN REALMS OF SILVER LAKE (Paranormal Romance)

Poppy (book 1)

Primrose (book 2)

Acacia (book 3)

Magnolia (book 4)

Box Set (books 1-4)

Jace (book 5)

Tanner (book 6)

WERES AND WITCHES OF SILVER LAKE (Paranormal Romance)

A Magical Shift (book 1)
Catching Her Bear (book 2)
Surge of Magic (book 3)
The Bear's Forbidden Wolf (book 4)
Her Reluctant Bear (book 5)
Freeing His Tiger (book 6)
Protecting His Wolf (book 7)
Waking His Bear (book 8)
Melting Her Wolf's Heart (book 9)
Her Wolf's Guarded Heart (book 10)
His Rogue Bear (book 11)
Box Set (books 1-4)
Box Set (books 5-8)
Reawakening Their Bears (book 12)

PACK WARS (Paranormal Romance)

Training Their Mate (book 1)
Claiming Their Mate (book 2)
Rescuing Their Virgin Mate (book 3)
Box Set (books 1-3)
Loving Their Vixen Mate (book 4)
Fighting For Their Mate (book 5)
Enticing Their Mate (book 6)
Box Set (books 1-4)
Complete Box Set (books 1-6)

HIDDEN HILLS SHIFTERS (Paranormal Romance)

An Unexpected Diversion (book 1)

Bare Instincts (book 2)

Shifting Destinies (book 3)

Embracing Fate (book 4)

Promises Unbroken (book 5)

Bare 'N Dirty (book 6)

Hidden Hills Shifters Complete Box Set (books 1-6)

MONTANA PROMISES (Full length contemporary Romance)

Promises of Mercy (book 1)

Foundations For Three (book 2)

Montana Fire (book 3)

Montana Promises Box Set (books 1-3)

Hart To Hart (Book 4)

Burning Seduction (Book 5)

Montana Promises Complete Box Set (books 1-5)

ROCK HARD, MONTANA (contemporary romance novellas)

Montana Desire (book 1)

Awakening Passions (book 2)

PLEDGED TO PROTECT (contemporary romantic suspense)

From Panic To Passion (book 1)

From Danger To Desire (book 2)

From Terror To Temptation (book 3)

Pledged To Protect Box Set (books 1-3)

BURIED SERIES (contemporary romantic suspense)

Buried Alive (book 1)

Buried Secrets (book 2)

Buried Deep (book 3)

The Buried Series Complete Box Set (books 1-3)

A NASH MYSTERY (Contemporary Romance)

Sidearms and Silk(book 1)

Black Ops and Lingerie(book 2)

A Nash Mystery Box Set (books 1-2)

STARTER SETS (Romance)

Contemporary

Paranormal

Author Bio

Love it HOT and STEAMY? Sign up for my newsletter and receive MONTANA DESIRE for FREE. smarturl.it/o4cz93?IQid=MLite

OR Are you a fan of quirky PARANORMAL COZY MYSTERIES? Sign up for this newsletter. smarturl.it/CozyNL

Not only do I love to read, write, and dream, I'm an extrovert. I enjoy being around people and am always trying to understand what makes them tick. Not only must my romance books have a happily ever after, I need characters I can relate to. My men are wonderful, dynamic, smart, strong, and the best lovers in the world (of course).

My Paranormal Cozy Mysteries are where I let my imagination run wild with witches and a talking pink iguana who believes he's a real sleuth.

I believe I am the luckiest woman. I do what I love and I have a wonderful, supportive husband, who happens to be hot!

Fun facts about me

(1) I'm a math nerd who loves spreadsheets. Give me numbers and I'll find a pattern.

(2) I live on a Costa Rica beach!

(3) I also like to exercise. Yes, I know I'm odd.

I love hearing from readers either on FB or via email (hint, hint).

Social Media Sites

Website:
www.velladay.com

FB:
facebook.com/vella.day.90

Twitter:
@velladay4

Gmail:
velladayauthor@gmail.com

Made in the USA
Las Vegas, NV
05 July 2021

25936887R00121